THE GHOST WRITER

SHADOWS OF THE PAST

MARTIN VAN HELDEN

ISBN: 978-1-922784-74-2 (Trade paperback)

A Catalogue record of this book is available from the National Library of Australia.

Self-Published by Martin van Helden, with assistance from Clark & Mackay

Dear Reader, ____

Congratulations on your purchase and many thanks from me Author
Martin van Helden and my team.

I have created all these stories and like to take you on this special
journey all through this interesting mysterious Thriller. (series)

Reading can be very enjoying and relaxing and you can take your
book wherever you go at any time of the day.

I hope you will enjoy this book and be inspired to look at my other
books to.

With the highest respect,

Martin van Helden.
Author

Martin van Helden would like to bring a huge thanks to all
the many people who were involved in making this book.

PROLOGUE

YEAR 2000

THE SUN WAS just descending below the horizon as the brown-haired woman in a gray sedan turned off the highway and onto a broad dirt road. She brushed a stray strand of hair behind an ear and sighed deeply. The woman blinked, struggling against sleep and exhaustion. The sharp tune of her Nokia phone jarred her to alertness. The woman gritted her teeth, refusing to reach for the phone that was nestled in her purse. She was pretty sure she knew who was calling and just like earlier in the day, she was in no mood to speak to them. She had already told them all she had to say. There was no turning back. And even when they had called her repeatedly after she walked out on them, she had told them point blank that she would not be doing their bidding. Why were they so dense that they could not get the message? Was it so hard to understand? She was pretty sure she had been as clear as possible.

The woman pulled up in front of a magnificent mansion that glistened under the stars that were starting to dot the darkening night sky. For a second, she stayed seated behind the wheel, staring at the building. Smile, she told herself. He always knew when something was wrong. She could not let him know how bothered she was. The woman shook her head. It was going to be hard, but she had to try so as not to worry him.

The woman grabbed her bag, just as her cellphone started ringing again. She grunted as she pulled her phone out.

"We have nothing else to talk about," she said decisively. "Please stop calling me. I already told you everything I had to when you supposedly 'ran' into me earlier, an occurrence I still refuse to buy."

She heard a snicker from the other end which was followed by a gravelly voice. "Do not think you know it all, young lady. We are still being very nice, so why don't you accept our good will? This will be the last time we ask this nicely."

"Look, there is nothing you can do that will convince me to do otherwise. If I was going to be convinced, I would have come to you asking for an incentive to do that. But I didn't. That should tell you I need nothing from you. I have no clue how you found out about this but I need you to realize that nothing you say or do will stop me. Now, stop bothering me."

"You clearly don't know who we are," The volume of the voice was increasing.

"And you also do not know who I am, because if you do, you would realize that all you are doing right now is not going to work."

"Oh, we know exactly know who you are. Your reputation certainly precedes you. We found out about this nonsense that you are about to do, despite all your efforts to keep it under wraps. That should tell you how powerful we are. And we are not to be trifled with. I am going to assume that it is your ignorance that makes you think this is a path that you can afford to walk on, but I promise you that it is not. Back away now."

"I will not. Now, stop bothering me." She hung up, interrupting his next words.

She hissed at her phone and threw it into her bag. How on earth had they actually gotten her number? She had been so surprised earlier in the day after she had left the plaza and immediately received a call from them? How had they even known she was there? She sighed and ran a hand through her hair. She had a ton of questions she would appreciate answered. The biggest question of them all was what had been nagging at her since they had first introduced themselves to her earlier that day, how on earth had they known about her and what she wanted to do? Who had told them everything? She had ensured to keep the circle as small as possible, and only few people knew of this, people she trusted greatly and had worked with time and time again. So, who could it have been?

The woman shook her head. She would not think about it now. She would have a shower, have a good meal, then she would give herself time to think. Yes, that would be it.

She unlocked the door and quietly let herself in. As she slipped in through the grand door, she heard a soft sound like footsteps. The woman turned around, her eyes darting around. Asides the road that led up to the house, the house was surrounded on all sides by woods. The woods at the rear of the house were not as dense because from the second floor, one could see the glistening lake which was accessible through a stone path that went through the woods. The area was not fenced in as the entire property was privately owned.

She saw nothing and shook the thought out of her head. She was just being paranoid because of those accursed people and the call she had just had. They were perfectly safe out there. Besides, only few people knew she was out here. It was okay.

The entrance foyer was dim due to the rays of light filtering in from the living room. She shrugged out of her boots and slipped on her slippers. The woman stifled a yawn as she walked farther into the room. Her eyes darted around. Where was he? He was usually there to pull her into a hug the moment she returned. Her eyes caught a note on the coffee table.

Down at the deck! The fireflies are coming down today! I will bring them home for you! I will be back before 8, don't worry! I LOVE YOU!

She chuckled and said softly, "I love you too."

Smiling, the woman headed to her room for the shower she had been longing for. About twenty minutes later, she emerged from the bathroom feeling much better after washing off the exhaustion the day had left her with. She pulled her hair into a ponytail and headed to the kitchen.

It was just seven-twenty. She would work on dinner before he arrived. The woman fixed a record on the turntable and placed the tonearm in position. As the familiar sound of *Call the Man* from Celine Dion's *Falling Into You* filled the room, the woman sang along. She headed to the kitchen island and got to work slicing the carrots, singing along as Celine belted the notes.

On the other side of the walls, two shadows moved away from the windows, tucking themselves by the sides of the front door. One of them gently slipped a pin into the door and in seconds, the door gently swung open. The shadows slipped in just as footsteps approached the foyer.

As she moved closer to the foyer, the woman wiped her hands on a napkin. She thought she had heard the sound of the front door, which was weird. He always used the back door as he did not like tracking dirt through the house. He never wanted to bother her. The foyer was still dim. She shook her head as she turned around. She must have imagined it. The music had been quite loud. She headed to the kitchen but then, froze in her tracks at the sight of the person seated calmly at the kitchen counter.

The woman swallowed hard. "Who are you and what do you want?"

The man smiled, a smile that did not reach his eyes, "They were right about you, you know, bold and defiant, even in the face of danger. Unfortunately, this world does not need more people like you. Do you understand?"

"I don't know what you mean. What I want is that you leave my house right now."

The man snickered. The woman felt terror run through her spine and she swallowed hard. She steeled herself as she glared at him.

"People like you are a nuisance to people like me, you know. How do we get things done if there are people like you who refuse to accept the status quo and just leave things as they are? Why do you want to dig up things you should not unearth? Why are you running around asking questions you should not?"

The woman swallowed hard and said softly but firmly, "Clearly, someone sent you here. The question is who."

"You have stepped on a lot of toes, huh? It certainly does not surprise me. you look like the kind of person who gets into a lot of trouble."

She heard footsteps and turned around to see two darkly dressed men. She swallowed again. This was no warning, she knew that for sure. They had come here with a mission. Her eyes flew to the clock over the kitchen stove. It was already seven-forty-five. She blinked back the tears that were threatening to spill.

Please, please, she whispered quietly, looking up, *he should not have to see this, please. Let them do as they want and leave before he returns. Please, keep him safe. Let him go untouched.*

"What? Cat got your tongue, lady?" The first man said, snarling.

"Do as you will and get out of here please," She replied through gritted teeth. They would hurt him too, she knew they would. They were ruthless, and she could smell the blood on his breath. She knew there was no way she could get out of this, so all she could pray for was that he got out unscathed.

The man chuckled as he stood up to open her refrigerator. "Ooh… you have a great array of drinks here."

The woman took advantage of the distraction to slide to the back door and immediately turn the knob, locking the door from the inside, and preventing entrance.

The man turned to her in that moment and grabbed her by her hair. She struggled against him and hissed, "I pity you and the life you lead."

"You really are a smart mouth," the man said and in a quick motion, he buried a knife in her belly. The woman gasped and held the handle of the knife, struggling as he pushed it deeper. She tried to hold on to the edge of the island but she slipped to the cold tile floor.

The men with him started cackling as the man whispered to her, "In your next life, you should learn not to step on the toes of those who can end you."

As the man stood up, her eyes rested on the glass back door where she could see him, looking on in horror and shock. He was struggling to open the door, tears rolling down his cheeks. The men turned at that moment and their leader hissed.

"Well, well, well… who do we have here?"

"Run! Run! Don't look back!" She managed to scream with the last bit of strength in her. A tear rolled down her cheek as one of the other two kicked her stomach, pushing the knife further into her stomach, completely burying the handle of the knife.

"What are you two fools still doing standing there? Get that bastard! He better not get away, else it will be your head on a pike." The leader screamed at his two henchmen.

The leader turned to her just as the men ran out the back-door. He snarled and whispered in the ear of the dying woman, "That sonofabitch is dead, just as you are."

"Please, don't…" she whispered, as blood pooled around her and her life seeped out of her. She tried to hold on to the man's jacket. "Please.…"

"Ah… where is the bravado you had just moments ago?" He smirked.

"Please…" The sound of a gunshot rented the night sky and the man threw his head back as he laughed.

"I never leave my jobs uncompleted," he winked.

"No…" she whispered, a tear rolling down her cheek. Her hand fell to her side and she went lifeless.

"Good riddance." The man spat out, and he headed out the door.

CHAPTER ONE

2023

DOMINIC GRAY WAS buried over his laptop, his fingers flying across his keyboard. Occasionally, his spiel stopped as he reached for his cup of coffee. A sip after, and he was back to work. The man was oblivious to the time until he was jolted by the sharp ringing sound from his phone. He ignored the first couple of rings, but the annoying sound returned almost immediately.

Dominic groaned as he ran a hand through his tousled brown hair. He peeked at the caller ID just before answering the call.

"Yes, Makayla? This better be quick."

"Do you not know what today is?" His publicist's voice floated to him.

"The day I am determined to work without distractions? Of course, I know what today is. And do you also know that you are ruining the day for me?"

He heard her exasperated sigh, just before she said, "Dominic, I guess you have forgotten. Well, it is a good thing I called then."

"Whatever it is you called to remind me about, it is clearly not important, seeing how I forgot about it."

"Today is the Literary Royalty Awards Night, Dominic. You know, the award event where you are receiving an award? Do you remember now? Do you realize how important this is, Dominic?" He could hear how much she was trying to reel in her impatience in her voice and it only made the man chuckle.

"I do not have to be there, right? I am sure you can just take the award for me, Makayla. Thank you, you are the best."

"Dominic, don't you dare hang up! Do you not realize how important this is?"

He sighed and leaned back in his soft paved chair. It was becoming clearer to him that the conversation was not going to end anytime soon. The man shrugged and said, "There really is no difference between this and the others, Makayla. Just take it for me. There is no need to make a fuss about this."

Dominic lifted his head and chuckled. He was in that moment staring at an entire wall of his million dollar mansion overlooking the sea which held all the awards he had received in his literary career and before. He had never been after the accolades and so there had never been a time he had freaked out over the showers of wins, and praises, not even when he first started in this world.

"I will not let you do this, Dominic. Do you know what they are saying about you? Many of them think you are full of yourself, and think yourself too big to mingle with the others in this industry. That is not a good look."

"It is only a particular sect saying that. They have been saying it from the very moment I started out, Makayla. They literally called me, 'a small fry trying to struggle against the sharks', and they made bets about how long I would survive. They all lost their bets, that's for sure. Anyway, the so-called industry giants do not respect others, so why then are they worthy of my respect?"

"Come on, Dominic. I do get where you are coming from, and trust me, I understand. You certainly have soared way above their expectations, and with the spotlight on you, they are ready to nitpick your every action. This is the biggest literary event of the year. Trust me, it won't look good if you are not present."

"I do not write for them, Makayla, I do not see why I have to look good for them."

"Dom…" Makayla started but Dominic quickly interrupted her

"Come on, Makayla. surely, you are tired of this song and dance that we do every single time there is an award show. Just collect it like you have always done, all right?"

"But…"

"Bye, Makayla. I will see you on Monday." The man rolled his eyes and turned back to his computer. He really had no idea when Makayla would finally get the message. They had worked together for three years already.

The man turned back to his laptop and frowned. Now, he had lost his train of thought. He groaned. He never should have answered that call. It was all for naught. Just an absolute waste of his time and mental energy. Dominic stood up and stretched his hands above his head.

Once he retrieved a bag of chips from his big luxurious kitchen, he settled in front of the 120" big television with a glass of orange juice. He flipped through the channels searching for something that would catch his attention, and spur him to continue working. Dominic quirked a brow when he saw the flash of lights at a red-carpet event.

"They sure are early," he murmured as he took a bite of a chip. His invitation had said the event would start at 9pm and it was just 7pm. Well, their red-carpet parade most likely started earlier, he concluded, else, how else would they get to prance around flaunting how much they could spend on an attire they would most likely wear only once in their life? The red-carpet show was a cannot miss for a great number of his fellow authors.

Dominic groaned tiredly as his phone started ringing again. It had to be Makayla. she was the only one who would disturb him this much on such a day. Jeez, the woman found it so hard to accept a 'No'. he could not understand why she was stressing the issue. It was not the first time she was collecting an award for him and it would most likely not be the last. They had a great dynamic and he really could not be bothered with things that he did not care about.

Dominic was determined not to leave the house. His phone kept ringing repeatedly, but he continued to ignore it. He checked the time and saw that it was almost 8:00 p.m.

"What to do? What to do?" he murmured. *Maybe I should just get some sleep*, he thought to himself.

The man grinned as he stood up. He would try to catch some sleep for a few hours, and he was bound to wake up feeling rejuvenated. He was halfway out of the room when his doorbell rang. The smile slipped off Dominic's face and he froze. He did not want to open that door as he felt that on the other side was trouble. Why was it so hard for him to catch a break? Frowning, he walked towards his intercom. Dominic rolled his eyes when he saw who was on the other side of the door. At this point in time, he would not be surprised if Makayla sent him.

With a sigh, he pulled the door open and before his best friend could say anything, Dominic said, "No, I will not be going, Harrison. There is absolutely nothing you are going to say that will convince me to go so go back and tell Makayla that you failed on this mission."

"Really? So you won't even let me come in? You are so impolite today, my friend, very impolite." Harrison shook his head.

Dominic rolled his eyes and stepped away from the door. "The fact that I am letting you in does not change anything, you know that, right?"

"What really is the big deal if you go for the event?"

"You and your wife are the ones turning it into a big deal," Dominic told him in a matter-of-fact tone. "I have a lot to do and the last place I want to be at is some stuffy event for the crème de la crème of the society, so I would appreciate if we end this conversation now. Thank you very much."

"Are you sure about that? Do you really want to deprive us, your loved ones, the opportunity to see you go up that stage and receive that award?"

Dominic quirked a brow, "What on earth are you talking about? My mother and sisters are not even in town at the moment, neither is Angelica, and I do not plan to go on stage to receive an award so you can have stars in your eyes, my good friend."

"Are you sure about that?" Harrison asked. He had a knowing look on his face.

"Hmmm... what are you not telling me, Harrison? What do you mean by that question?" Dominic asked his friend.

"Well... you seem very convinced that there's nobody who wants to see you go up on that stage besides me, who you seem not to care so much about. Does that mean if there was someone extremely special who wanted to see you go up on that stage, you would go?"

"Why do I feel like you are about to trick me into doing something I do not want to do?"

"You still haven't answered the question, my friend," an amused Harrison said.

"And you still have not answered my question."

"Well if you must know, Angelica is on her way to the venue from the airport," Harrison announced with a flourish.

"What? That is not true. She won't be back for the next couple of weeks." Dominic shook his head defiantly. He refused to be deceived.

Harrison clapped him on the back as he said, "That is what you think. For your information, my friend, Angelica heard about tonight and she is returning to surprise you. She wanted to be there to cheer for you when you go up on the stage and give your speech."

Dominic sighed and ran a hand through his silky hair, "Why would Angelica do that? She knows how I feel about these award events."

"Why else? Because of how big and important tonight is. Deny it all you want, my friend, but the truth remains that the Literary King award is a gigantic feather on your cap. Yes, you have won a lot of awards in the past, but this award, it is huge my friend. I really do not think you should take it for granted. Angelica recognizes that and that is why she came back to be present for you today. She thought you would feel the same way but clearly you do not."

"I really do not like to be pressured to do what I do not want to do, man. I can think of a thousand and one things I would rather do tonight, and none of them includes that event."

"Why don't you tell that to your girlfriend?" Harrison chuckled.

Dominic narrowed his eyes, "You know what? I do not believe you. I am going to call her and see what she says."

"Be my guest," Harrison said with a shrug.

"And if this is a joke, trust me, I will not find it funny, but rather, I will consider it a waste of my precious time," Dominic muttered as he speed dialed his girlfriend.

"Yeah, whatever," his friend said as he made his way to the kitchen. "Do you have any good food in there? I hope you do because I am super famished."

"You and your wife could not get some food because you were too busy bothering me?" Dominic threw at him as he waited for Angelica to answer the phone.

"Hi babe!" her breathless voice came on.

Dominic narrowed his eyes, "Where are you, love?"

"Uh… me? I'm uh… in… the hotel, about to…"

"You are on your way to the event center, aren't you? You are back in town," Dominic shook his head.

"Oh come on! How did you know? Harrison or Makayla? It was supposed to be a surprise! Why did they ruin it?" He could hear her pout.

Dominic sighed, "Babe, why? You said you would not be back for the next two weeks, and you still have work, and you know how I feel about these things."

"I wanted to be here for you babe, so I rounded up early. Aren't you excited that I am back?" she asked softly.

"Of course I am. You know I am. You do not need to ask that. But you know how I feel about these award events. I do not give a hoot about them."

"Yes, yes, I know that, but this is really big, Dom. You are being crowned the Literary king of the year. Next time, you will be crowned the King of the Decade! Can you not see how big this is, my love?"

"I am sorry to say that I am not as excited as you are," Dominic said with a shrug.

"Please, babe, I really want to see you go up there! I want to scream at the top of my lungs for you. Can you do it? Just this one time, please?"

He sighed, "Babe, you know I don't…"

"Pretty please? Come on, do it for me? Huh? I will see you at the venue, right? I love you, Dom."

She hung up before he could reply. Dominic let out a sigh and his hand holding his phone fell to the side. Harrison emerged from around the corner, his eyes glinting with amusement, and wielding a bag of crackers.

"Told you. You thought I was playing you, didn't you?"

"Right now, I dislike you a great deal, man."

Harrison grinned, "You and I know that is not true. so, what are you waiting for, Dominic? Chop, chop, you got to get ready. I know you are the star of the show but that does not mean you should be late. Well, if you are fashionably late, it is not so bad though."

"Where did you find my pea crackers?" Dominic frowned at his friend.

Harrison shrugged, "I raided your snack bar, durrh. You know, it is so sad how you have an entire shelf filled with snacks and junk food, standing next to a gigantic double doored refrigerator devoid of everything but bottled water. I do not know why you do not have some pizza, wings or beer in there, man. What do you use your money for?"

"First and foremost, snacks are easy and not a nuisance, like you are being right now," Dominic said pointedly "Secondly. If you want to drink a beer, go to your house and drink a beer. This is my house, and that's my kitchen so I stock it with whatever I want, not what you want, my good friend. Thirdly, stay away from my snacks, man. They were perfectly curated to fit my palate needs at different times."

"Yeah, whatever. Go get ready, now. Shoo, shoo, I will call Makayla and let her know that we will meet her at the event."

Dominic rolled his eyes, "Yeah whatever."

He headed toward the stairs and paused to ask, "Did you drive down? We can just go in your car."

"Oh, no can't do, man. I need to take Makayla to the hospital after the event."

"Oh? Is she okay?" an alarmed Dominic asked.

"Oh yes, just visiting family, and I have to be there as the favorite in-law."

"Yeah, I get that. I will just drive then. Or what if I just take a cab? I can just return with Angelica. Yeah, that works. She probably retrieved her car from the airport parking lot. What? Why are you looking at me that way?"

"The woman just got off a six-hour flight? Do you really want her to drive you home as well after a long day? Cut her some slack, my man." Harrison shook his head, a reproachful look on his face.

"Fine, fine. Jeez. I will drive myself. You exhaust me," Dominic groaned and turned away, leaving his laughing friend behind.

They pulled up with his gray Range Rover as the porter took his car there was a large crowd gathered outside, the lights whare smoothly shining on the elegant red carpet.

Dominic smart dressed with black tuxedo walked into the large event hall with Harrison, his eyes darting around for Angelica. He found her at a table with Makayla. Angelica pulled him into a tight hug,

"I missed you, babe." she said softly.

"I missed you too, my love." He replied. "Well, I think it is obvious enough, considering the fact that I am here, where I do not want to be."

She threw her head back and laughed, "Oh stop being such a crybaby, my love. We are going to have a lot of fun, I promise you."

"Yeah, I do not see that happening." Dominic rolled his eyes.

"Forever the pessimist," Makayla said with a slight shake of her head.

"How was your flight, my love?"

Before Angelica could respond, Dominic heard his name. He forced a smile and turned around to see the caller.

"Wow, wow, wow, do my eyes deceive me? Is this really Dominic Gray standing before me?" a man with thinning black hair said. He was flanked on both sides by two younger men.

"Have you begun to have visual hallucinations? I am very sorry to hear about that. It is such a shame indeed," Dominic said in the politest voice he could muster.

The man gritted his teeth and he said, "I can see you have not lost that unique sense of humor you possess, Dominic."

"Oh, I did not realize my sense of humor bothered you. Weren't you just on the morning show three weeks ago talking about how much you appreciate my unique sense of humor? Oh, and how we are good colleagues?"

"Oh, but of course we are. Have you forgotten that we go way back?"

"How can I possibly forget? You are one of the gatekeepers of the literary world, aren't you? And you definitely did everything possible to keep me out when I first started. It was all to no avail, of course, because I am standing right here. It is not easy to forget about you, Charles. I am sure a lot of people in this room agree with me as well."

One of the men with Charles stepped forward, but Charles put a hand in front of him holding him back.

"It is nice seeing you again, after such a long time, Dominic. And congratulations on the award. I hope you have a great time tonight. I expect to see you around some more."

"Thank you for your kind wishes," Dominic said quietly. He quirked a brow, wondering what he meant by seeing him more.

As the man walked away, they heard the man that had been held back complaining to Charles, saying, "How could you let him talk to you that way? He had no right. You should have let me teach him a lesson or two."

"Are they for real?" Angelica gasped. "It is clear he is so jealous of you, my love."

Dominic chuckled and shrugged, "I really don't care. Is this thing going to start anytime soon?"

"Good vibes, Dom, good vibes. I know it is not easy, but good vibes only. Remember that Charles is a very important person in this community. You do not want to get on his bad side." Harrison patted his hand and winked, causing Dominic to roll his eyes.

As the evening filled with entertainment, rich china and fine dining went on.

Several minutes later ……."My man! Dominic Gray!" Someone exclaimed from behind Dominic. He sighed and turned around. This time, a genuine smile spread across his face as he set his eyes on an old friend from college.

"Wesley! It has been so long! Wait, aren't you supposed to be in the UK?" Dominic shook hands with him. He smiled and nodded his head at the woman beside Wesley as Angelica moved closer to him.

"Oh, I have been back for a couple of months now. You are looking at the new Chief Publisher of Hidden Secrets." Wesley, a man who matched Dominic's six foot, five inches, grinned as he spread his arms.

"Whoa, that is really huge. Congratulations are in order then!"

"Thank you, man. You know, I tried reaching out to you but I could find no one who had your contact information. Of course, it was not surprising not to get your contact from any of our class-mates. You never really mingled with a lot of them. But, I thought I would be able to get it from your publishing company, but I kept hitting a wall as no one agreed to speak with me." Wesley explained.

"Really? I apologize for that. I truly had no idea about it," Dominic stared pointedly at Makayla who averted her gaze and took a sip of her wine. He turned back to Wesley and said, "I should give it to you now, and we definitely need to catch up one of these days."

"Yes, please."

The two men exchanged their business cards just as Angelica cleared her throat and said, "Babe, aren't you going to introduce me to your friend?"

"Right, where are my manners? Wesley, this is Angelica, my girlfriend. Angelica, meet Wesley, a good friend from college."

"It is nice to meet you." Wesley said quietly. He introduced the woman next to him as his wife and the small group exchanged pleasantries as Dominic went on to introduce Harrison and Makayla.

"Ah, the publicist…" Wesley said with a slow nod.

"My apologies about that. Dominic is a very private person and we try our best not to give his information to just anyone."

"Sure… I understand that…" Wesley said slowly. He turned back to Dominic and said. "Alexandria and I are in New York for this event and some conferences. We should be heading back to Massachusetts by next weekend. It would be nice if we can meet up for dinner or something before we leave."

"I think that is a great idea. We can plan something and even now that you live, what four, five hours away? It would be great if we can see each other more often," Dominic was saying when Angelica interrupted,

"Be careful making so many promises, my love. Remember you are very busy. You do not have the time to hang out with any Tom, Dick or Harry."

Silence loomed for a second, silence that was interrupted by Alexandria's scoff. She opened her mouth to speak but Dominic beat her to it, "It is true that I am busy, but I can never be too busy for true friends."

Wesley smiled and his wife's face visibly softened.

"You really have not changed, Dom. It is amazing. Your name is literally a household name but you are still the unbothered Dom from back then who does not give a hoot about all of these." Wesley waved his hand around.

Dominic grinned, "Is it very obvious how uncomfortable I feel here?"

"Only in the eyes of those who know you," Wesley smiled. "And congratulations on your award, my friend. That is no easy feat."

"Thank you, that is really all I can say because…"

"We cannot just stand here all night talking to your friends, babe. We need to actually mingle and interact with others," Angelica interrupted.

Dominic sighed and before he could speak, Alexandria said, "It was really nice meeting you, Dom. Wesley has told me a lot about you, and I can see that none of it was exaggerated."

The woman looked Angelica over, and the latter glared at her. Alexandria shook her head slightly and said, "We have some more people to meet so we will get out of your hair now. Right, Wes?"

"Right. Let's meet up soon, Dom." Wesley said and the men shook hands again.

As soon as they were out of earshot, Dominic turned to Angelica, "Really? What on earth was that for, Angelica? That is a friend I have not seen in a long time and you acted that way."

"He is just a publisher, Dom, of Hidden Secrets? What stance does that publication have among celebrities like us?" She asked.

"And so what? What does that have to do with anything? And wait a minute, I am no celebrity."

"You are an award-winning author. You should not be seen with the likes of him. You need to change your circle. I keep telling you this."

"I beg your pardon?" Dominic blinked hard, stunned by what he had just heard.

"I agree with Angelica, Dom. He was your friend in the past, cool, that does not mean you have to be in the same circle with him now," Makayla chipped in. Harrison nodded beside her.

"Interesting…. Is that why you blatantly refused to tell me anything about him reaching out?"

"I…" She started but Dominic was not done.

"How many more people have you prevented me from interacting with because of this ridiculous image you are trying to keep up, Makayla?"

"Come on, Dom, we only want what is best for you. You are one of the biggest stars of the publishing house and you do not expect us to let you roll around with just about anyone. You are a king and you should not be seen with the peasants."

Dominic nodded slowly, "You are the owner of the publishing company, Harrison, and Makayla, you are my publicist. But first and foremost, both of you are my friends. When did it become just about money and image with you both? How come I never saw it?"

"Oh stop being so dramatic, Dom. We just want the best for you," Angelica rolled her eyes.

"You are just like most people in this industry and I have just been too blind. The fact that I am here right now, against my own will proves it." He shook his head.

"Angelica is right, Dom, you are blowing this out of proportion and refusing to see the perspective. The simple truth is you are a star, you need to understand this and know that the players you despise, such as Charles are the one you should be interacting with from now henceforth, do you understand that?"

"So changing myself to fit a persona that you all have created. Interesting… It is very funny and interesting because you of all people, Harrison know how much I appreciate genuineness and truth," Dominic nodded slowly. He picked up the glass of wine he had set on the cocktail table and took a sip. As he looked around at all the people drinking, and dancing on the shiny, polished floor, and the spectacularly elegant set up, he turned and smiled at them and said, "Clearly, we all have a lot to talk about when this party is over. I can see that we are all no longer on the same page and changes will have to be made going forward."

"What does that mean?" Harrison's eyes flashed with anger.

"Why don't we talk about this later? We don't want to ruin the party for anyone, do we?" Dominic downed his wine, set the glass on the table and headed in the other direction, leaving the three of them with their mouths open.

CHAPTER TWO

DOMINIC NODDED HIS thanks at the valet parking and slipped into his car. He fastened his seatbelt and the gray Range Rover headed into the busy traffic. His eyes drifted to the plaque that was on the seat beside him and he sighed. He shook his head and focused on the road. It had certainly been a very eventful evening and what he longed for at that moment was the hot shower he was so deprived of earlier in the day.

He shook his head, refusing to think about what transpired between him, Harrison, Makayla and Angelica. He had avoided them for the rest of the night, and Angelica had gotten her chance to scream at the top of her lungs when he stepped up to receive the award. He rolled his eyes. He had no idea who he was more pissed at right now. After leaving them, he had put a call through to the publishing company and found out he had been booked for a series of promotion events all involving those so-called big players. His grip around the steering wheel tightened as he tried to hold back his anger. When were they planning to tell him about all of it? No wonder Charles was confident he would be seeing him around.

Dominic shook his head. It was not just about the fact that those people made life difficult for him when he started out, and for budding writers. It was not only because they were bullies. It went way beyond that. They were scummy, dirty, all shades of corrupt and those he considered dear to him were supposed to know how much he did not want to associate with those people.

He sighed. What really had been their grand plan? How had they planned to get him to participate in those events? Well... the only answer he could think about was, clearly by lying and manipulating him. He shook his head again, he was not going to think about all of that now. He would get home, have a relaxing night, and make a decision with a clear head in the morning. Yes, that was what he would do.

Dominic suddenly winced, as a sharp pain shot through his left arm. He tried to lift it but it suddenly felt weak. He groaned as a sickening warmth enveloped him. Alarm rang in his head. He had no idea what was going on but he had to get off the road and call for help. He stepped on the brakes but they failed.

"Oh crap." Dominic muttered. With his one good hand, he managed to stretch out his hand for his car navigation system.

Dominic's eyes widened when he saw a truck in front of him. He pressed the brakes again but they failed once more. He managed to swerve just as he felt the pain sharpen.

"Siri, call 911…" he strangled out. "I think I am having a heart attack."

"Calling emergency services…" The soft mechanical voice of the AI assistant was the last thing he heard before Dominic blacked out. As he faded away, Dominic was oblivious to the crashing sounds or the glass that shattered around him. As the car rolled over multiple times it came to a hold on the sight of the road badly smoking and hissing.

~

Dominic's gray eyes blinked open and he found himself staring at bright lights. He winced as he tried to raise his hand to his throbbing head. *Where am I?* was the first thought that ran through his head. He struggled to breathe and saw that there was something in his nose. He started flailing as he heard the beeping of machines and a scream.

After what seemed like forever, a soothing voice said, "Welcome back, Mr. Gray."

The tube in his nose was removed and he felt instant relief as he breathed through his nose.

"Wh…" his voice came out raspy, and slowly his bed was tilted a little and he had a better view of his surroundings. He was in a hospital room.

"Please do not try to speak so much. You have been under nasotracheal intubation for a long time. It is normal to have a sore throat." The man who he could now see clearly patted his shoulder. "Thank you for coming back to us, Mr. Gray."

Dominic swallowed and slowly, he looked around. His memories were still fuzzy. "I… I don't remember much…. Just… the accident."

"That is normal also. You were in a coma for a couple of months, Mr. Gray. It will all come back to you. We have been monitoring you with regular tests and there is no swelling in your brain. Nonetheless, we will carry out another test today. But at this time, there is nothing to worry about."

"Two… two months?" He stuttered.

"Yes, I am sorry. But let's look at the positive, right? You are alive. And your family is waiting for you."

Dominic shut his eyes tight as his mother's face popped into his head. He could not imagine how horrible she must have felt in the past months. And his sisters! He shuddered. They must have been so devastated. What of Angelica? He sighed. He opened his eyes and said,

"I would like to see my family now. I don't want to keep them waiting any longer."

"Of course. As soon as we are done with all the tests, you will."

He nodded slowly. Life was really crazy. Two months unconscious? He had certainly never imagined this would happen.

A little while later, Dominic's mother and sisters were ushered into the room by a nurse. As soon as his mother saw him, she threw her arms around him and wailed profusely.

"Don't you ever do that again. Don't! What would we do if we lose you? You scared us so much! My poor baby!"

As his mother held on to him, Dominic saw a flash and it felt like Déjà vu. He swallowed hard, and held on to his mother.

"I'm sorry, mom," that was all Dominic could say.

His sisters threw their arms around him as well, and for a long time they all held on to each other. When his family finally let go of him, Dominic's eyes flitted over to the door. He had expectation written on his face as he waited for someone else to walk through the door.

"What are you looking for, Dominic?" Eva, his immediate younger sister asked.

"Angelica. Does she not know I am awake now? I guess you've not gotten around to telling her yet?" The moment he asked the question, Dominic noticed an exchange of glances between his mother and his sisters. "What is it? What are you not telling me? Is Angelica okay? She wasn't in the car, I know that for a fact. What are you all not telling me?"

"Dominic, I think we can talk about this another time," his mother started saying but he shook his head and said,

"No, mom. I would prefer if you tell me what is going on right now. Do not keep anything from me. Where is Angelica?"

"Dominic, you see..." his mother wrung her hands.

"She never came here to see you once, Dominic," his second sister Ana said. "I never liked that girl, but I chose to tolerate her because of you, brother, because you love her. I have lost track of the number of times I called her. Mom called her too and so did Eva but she ignored all our calls. She never came over here, and she never called. And she has no excuse whatsoever, mom and Eva have been amazing to her. You were amazing to her. She probably thought you were going to die. I bet she thought you were a lost cause, just like most of the others so she decided to count her chicks before they hatched. She bailed on you, brother."

"Ana! Come on! I am sure there is a reasonable explanation for her absence," Eva reproached her younger sister.

Ana scoffed, "Please do not be naïve, sister. You and I both know that she bailed on our brother. It's as simple as that. I mean, you've seen the news about her galivanting around town with that actor, right? Who knows how long they have been together? I bet you she was cheating on Dominic."

"Hush, child!" Their mother chided her. "Do you have no filter? Do you ever listen to yourself when you speak?"

Dominic forced a smile, "It is fine, mom. Thank you for being honest with me."

"Come on, Dom. You cannot be so sure that she left you. She might just be very busy or…" Eva sighed and ran a hand through her long brown hair.

Dominic shook his head, "See? You give everyone in the world the benefit of doubt, Eva, and you cannot even come up with a good enough excuse for her right now. That tells me all I need to know."

"But did you both have a fight or something? Did…"

Ana did not let her sister finish her words as she said, "Even if they argued, that does not mean she should ignore him for two months. If she could not come over, the least she could do was make a phone call. One minute would be enough to find out how Dom is doing but she simply did not care, Eva. Please, do not try to think up excuses for her."

"I am not, all right? I am not."

Dominic sighed and ran a hand over his face, "Something did happen the night of the accident but…"

"But what? Did you both break up?" his mother asked softly, her eyes heavy with concern.

"No, no, there was some issue. I will explain it to you all later."

"Does this something have anything to do with Harrison too?" Ana asked quietly.

"How do you…"

"Because not once has he or his dear wife come over here. They have been busy selling more of your books, and having candlelight concerts, in your name. It is pretty ironic seeing as they actually do not know your exact status. I bet they think the value of your books will skyrocket when you die and are waiting for the sad news," Ana hissed.

"Anastasia Gray! When will you ever learn to bridle your tongue, child?!" Their mother gasped.

Ana shrugged, "I am simply saying the truth, mom. I say the truth that everyone else is too scared to say."

"Oh, this child!"

The three siblings exchanged looks and Eva quickly reached out to their mother.

"Let's get you some food, mom. You have not eaten anything good in the past few hours. Who am I kidding? You have barely eaten since the accident. Come on."

"I don't want to leave your brother."

"Mom, it's fine. Ana is here with me. you should get something to eat, all right? Please?"

"Fine, but we should not take long," his mother told his sister sternly as she looked at her watch.

"Yes, mom." She nodded slowly.

His mother turned to him and pulled him into a tight embrace, "Thank you so much, my son. Thank you for coming back to us."

She stroked his silky hair and kissed his forehead before heading out. As soon as the two of them were out of the room, Ana turned to her brother and squeezed his hand.

"You gave us a big scare, big brother. Please, don't do this ever again."

He smiled softly and wiped the tears off her cheeks, "You've had to be so strong for mom. I know, and I am so sorry."

He pulled her into a hug as she let her tears fall. That was his baby sister. She was tough and would defend the ones she loved tooth and nail, but she was also a softie when it came to the ones she loved. Just as they were her weakness, they were also her strength. The three siblings had a tight-knit relationship and he hated to think of the horror they had all gone through in the past months. All he could think was how grateful he was that he got a second chance at life.

"So, are you going to tell me what happened at the party? Why were you even at that party? You never go to them. You absolutely despise them!"

Dominic sighed and gave his sister a breakdown of what he could remember about the night of his accident. He was realizing that the more he spoke, the clearer his memories became.

"So, let me get this straight. You only went to the event because of her, and she couldn't even…"

"No, no, don't blame her. No one could have predicted this would happen. I made the choice to go there, so don't put this on her, all right?"

"Fine, fine," she frowned. Silence loomed between them for a few moments, then she said, "The doctor said it was a heart attack."

Dominic nodded slowly. He shut his eyes tight as the events of the night replayed in his head. He had been so lucky to survive, and he would not take it for granted. "I was surprised too. I never expected to have one. I am just thirty-six!"

"We were surprised too! Anyway, I am so glad you had enough time to use Siri to call 911, I hate to think what would have happened if there had been any more delays."

Dominic sighed, "If only my brakes did not fail, I most likely would have not ended up in the accident though."

Ana's head flew up, "What do you mean? What are you talking about?"

He shrugged, "I just mean if I had been able to park my car, I would have been found by emergency services in one piece and the only issue that would have been addressed was the heart attack. But the fact that my brakes failed led to the accident." And "speaking off" where is my car?

It's in the towing company's yard for you to decide on it as it is a total write off.

"Your brakes failed? How is this the first time I am hearing about this?" the siblings looked up see their mother standing at the door, a look of horror on her face.

She wrung her hands together and paced the room, muttering repeatedly, "This is bad, this is bad."

"Mom, are you okay?" Eva touched her shoulder, jolting her out of her dazed state.

Their mother looked up at them. She looked surprised to see them.

"Mom, are you sure you should not get some sleep? These past few months have been really rough. You need some rest."

"Did you just hear what your brother said? They tried to kill him and they almost succeeded. What if they try again? What are we going to do then? What do we do?"

"Okay, mom. Please, calm down. No one said anything about it being an attempt on his life. It was a simple accident. He had a heart attack and..." Eva started.

"And he could not stop his car. Now tell me what does that tell you? It is clear that someone tampered with his brakes so that he could have an accident and die. And they would have succeeded if he had not had a heart attack. The heart attack caused him to call the emergency services early enough that they were able to get to him on time even after the accident that they planned out for him!" Their mother exclaimed, resuming her pacing.

"Okay, mom. I think you are being quite paranoid right now. Yes, accidents do not just happen but there are so many explanations for them. The car could have been faulty, it could have been anything else."

"I am not being paranoid!"

"Mom, you were married to a cop for so long, so it is understandable that you suspect every situation, but..." Eva started but her mother's glare caused her to go quiet.

"It is for the exact reason that I was a police detective's wife for so long, that I know when a situation is fishy," her mother retorted.

"Aren't you just making a mountain out of a molehill?" Eva sighed and turned to her siblings, "Come on, you guys, help me here."

"What if there is a possibility that mom is right? Can we really say 'never' with all certainty? I mean, the sweetest people in the world have enemies, right? What more our brother who is doing so well for himself and is definitely surrounded by people we cannot really consider the best kind of people. We have to be honest and admit that he has curated a set of enemies for himself. I am not saying it is true, but I am just saying that it is also not impossible."

"Exactly!"

"I do not know what I am going to do with both of you." Eva said and turned to her brother. Is there anything you would like to say?"

"About what?"

"About what we are talking about, of course," Eva said as she crossed her arms.

"Ah... if I have any opinion about the fact that someone might have tried to kill me? No, at this point in time, I really do not have any stance about the issue, but I will definitely get back to you on it. But right now, and what is priority to me in this moment, I can tell you that, if that is okay?"

"Yes, sure, of course, son. Tell us anything that you want. We will do everything that is in our power to get it for you," his mother squeezed his hands.

"As long as it is not Angelica, of course," Ana chipped in.

Eva groaned and ran a hand over her face. She poked her sister in her side, "You really need a filter for your mouth."

"Why filter the truth?" Ana asked in a tone that said she found that to be the most incredulous thing in the world.

"I would really like to sleep now, if that is okay." He said softly. He was beginning to feel very overwhelmed. He was sure it was normal though. He had been asleep for a very long time, right? It was probably normal to feel this way after not being active or out in the sun for a bit of time. This was an experience he would never wish on anybody, that was for sure.

"Of course! Can the both of you see what is happening? This isn't what he needs right now," Eva said in a matter-of-fact tone.

"Oh, I am so sorry baby, so sorry we stressed you out." his mother kissed his cheeks and held him tight. "Thank you so much, my baby."

"Are you going to be okay by yourself?" Ana asked him with a sad smile.

He smiled softly and said, "I am actually doing you all a favor. I'm getting rid of you before the doctor comes in and does the job himself."

"Okay, his crazy sense of humor is back. He's definitely going to be okay," Eva chuckled.

Just then, the door opened and the doctor from earlier who had introduced himself to Dominic as Dr. Perry stepped in. He was flanked by a nurse.

"Ah, just the person we were talking about," Dominic smiled ruefully.

"I did not realize you all were still here. I know you are very glad to see him, but he really needs his rest, so that means, shorter visiting time. Is that okay?" Dr. Perry asked the three women, in a soft, yet firm tone.

They nodded and expressed their gratitude. They headed out but Eva was back in almost immediately,

"Oh, I just remembered. There was a friend of yours who came to see you after the accident. Well, technically, many people have come to check on you after the accident, we can provide that list to you later," She giggled. "He just comes to mind right now because he calls mom pretty much every day to check on you."

"Oh, that is very true. I cannot believe we forgot about that." Ana nodded, popping up behind her sister.

"What was his name again?" Eva asked.

"Wesley, yes! Wesley!" Ana announced giddily.

"I see..." Dominic smiled at his sisters.

His doctor sighed and quirked a brow at them.

"Say no more, doc, we are leaving. But wait, can we at least show him the picture?" Not waiting for his response, Ana jumped into the room and to Dominic's side.

A confused Dominic found himself staring at a picture of a large room filled with flowers, balloons, and cards.

"What is going on...?"

"So many people have been sending them, your readers, colleagues, fans, so many people. They sent to the hospital but your doctor here said there was no way they could all fit in here so we took them home, and now, everyone else just sends to the café."

"Uh huh, we had a hard time accessing the patient due to all the presents," Dr. Perry reminded Ana. He jabbed a hand at the door.

"Fine, I will leave." She pouted and headed out.

Dominic chuckled, "I apologize. I hope you can understand."

Dr. Perry smiled, "Of course, I do. You have a beautiful family, and I am glad I got to give them the good news of your recovery."

"Thank you."

"You know what happened to you, right? A heart attack... yikes..."

"Uh huh..."

"There is a lot you need to do, Mr. Gray, and top of it is major lifestyle changes."

Dominic nodded slowly, "I cannot argue with you on that, doc. I really cannot."

CHAPTER THREE

DOMINIC STABBED THE cherry tomato with a fork and popped it into his mouth. He sighed as he pushed his plate away. The man reached for his class of freshly squeezed orange juice and washed his breakfast down. As he pulled away from the breakfast nook, many thoughts flooded his head. It had been his regular for the past couple of weeks. He reached for his phone and swiped up to his recorder.

"A man and woman trapped at sea, what happens when they have to survive with rations enough for just one person? Throw in the element of science fiction and we are left with a cacophony of elements. How will things play out?"

He ended the recording and sighed as he swiped through the folder of recordings. Since he woke up at the hospital some weeks ago till that moment, he had over 50 voice recordings. They were all story ideas. After what happened to him, he had made up his mind to take things easy. As much as he wanted to work, he needed to do the healthy thing for him. And a major healthy life decision was reducing his workload and taking a much-needed break. So at this point in time, when his hands were tied, what he could do was record all his story ideas for a day when he could finally start working on them.

Dominic slipped his phone into his pocket and headed to the specious living room. There was no point crying over spilled milk. He had come to realize that now. What he could do, was make the best of the situation he had found himself in. He was just going to see this as a long-anticipated vacation, a vacation he had not given himself the chance to go on for a really long time. It was unplanned, yes, but it was very necessary.

His doorbell rang at that moment but Dominic did not stand up. He had a feeling that the person at the door was an unwanted visitor. His mother and sisters knew his passcode, so they would never knock or ring the bell when they arrived. They always let themselves in. And considering the fact that he had not received a call from anyone about a visit, it was a wise conclusion that the person at the door was someone who was not wanted.

The ringing of the doorbell persisted, causing Dominic to roll his eyes in annoyance. He stood up and stalked over to the intercom. He scoffed when he saw who it was. Indeed people were shameless, like his sister Ana always said. While he was still contemplating the choice to open the door or not, Ana appeared behind Makayla. He could feel his sister's glare even though he was not the one it was targeted at and it was happening through several feet of concrete.

"What exactly can I help you with?" he heard his sister ask through the intercom.

"I would like to see Dominic," Makayla replied quietly.

He saw his sister quirk a brow as she crossed her arms and said, "What do you want from him? You certainly did not feel like seeing him when he was in the hospital. Now, you have bounced over here like you own the place."

"It is very good to see you again, Ana. It has been quite a while."

"Unfortunately, I cannot say the same thing about you," Dominic heard his sister say.

Okay, it was time. Chuckling under his breath, Dominic opened the door.

"Are you not supposed to be asleep?" Ana asked him, her frown deepening.

"Soon," he told his sister with a smile. "I had a late breakfast."

Dominic turned to Makayla, "Makayla, fancy seeing you here. Pray tell me, what it is you are doing here and what you want?"

She shrugged and said, "Is it so unusual to want to check on my friend?"

"It is unusual considering the fact that you never bothered calling while he was in the hospital. Why? Because you all thought that he would not survive, and did the first thing you could think of, cash in on his royalties."

"Okay, that is not true. I will not allow you speak to me as you very well please, Ana."

"Why? Does the truth bother you so much, Makayla? Whatever lies you came here to tell my brother, thank you for the attempt but we are not going to buy them. Unlike before, he is not going to fall hook, line and sinker so I advise that you stop trying while you are still ahead."

"Dom, are you really going to allow her talk to me this way?" Makayla asked incredulously, looking from one sibling to the other.

Dominic opened his mouth to retort but something stopped him. There was no use wasting anymore time. He already knew everything he needed to know and had been planning to go to the office. Since Makayla was already here, this was definitely the right time. He shook his head slightly and said, "Ana, please let her come in."

"But…" his sister started protesting but Dominic placed a hand on her shoulder.

"I was going to see her anyway," He whispered to his sister, "It is best to just do this and get it over with."

She looked very worried and he smiled reassuringly at her. Dominic backed away from the door, giving Makayla space to enter the house. Her eyes widened the moment she stepped in.

"Wow, I love what you have done with the place, Dominic. It looks so different. And it certainly feels airier. This is good. I cannot believe how you were able to pull it off, considering how you are."

"Did you come here to admire the change in my décor? I highly doubt that," Dominic said quietly.

"You look really good, Dom," Makayla said as moved farther into the living room. "I am happy to see it, and your friend Harrison will be equally happy."

Ana scoffed, "Yeah, right. I guess in your case, words speak louder than actions right?"

Dominic massaged his temple and sighed. He stretched a hand at a couch and said, "Please, sit."

"Thank you," she said with a smile and settled in.

Ana rolled her eyes and headed to the seat right across from Makayla so she could have a perfect view to glare at her.

"So, when did you get out of the hospital?" Makayla inquired.

"A few weeks ago," Dominic told her quietly.

"And you didn't tell us your friends? You didn't even tell Angelica? Come on, that was not fair of you, Dom. We are supposed to be your best buds." Makayla pouted.

From the corner of his eyes, Dom could see his sister rolling her eyes. He smiled softly and said to Makayla, "Gone are the days when you succeeded in gaslighting me, Makayla. You really should stop while you are ahead."

"I..." Her mouth clamped shut. He raised a brow, waiting for her excuse. Maybe, just maybe he could get something realistic from her. "Sorry we couldn't come over to the hospital, Dom. We were busy trying to keep your career afloat and..."

"By organizing candlelight concerts and selling more of my books and making the company more money, right? What was that thing you said again, Ana? Something about a dead talent having more value to these lots than an alive one?"

"Uh huh," his sister nodded slowly.

"That is not true, and you know it. We were looking out for you and trying to ensure that you do not get forgotten while you were down."

"Right... indeed that was very thoughtful of you guys. I mean, you did such great promotions, partnering with Charles and the likes. I should thank you then, right?" The man nodded slowly.

"Well, that would be nice," she chuckled.

"Indeed, sarcasm was always lost on you, Makayla. Maybe that should have been my first hint to run, but then, you guys were supposed to be my friends. I certainly did not expect these turn of events," Dominic said more to himself than to Makayla.

"I beg your pardon?" Makayla sat up in her seat.

Dominic clasped his hands together and said, "You can return to the company and tell Harrison that your mission was unsuccessful."

Makayla swallowed hard and leaned forward. She was now visibly tense. "I don't understand, Dom. What do you mean?"

"After news of my accident reached you along with the fact that I was in a coma, I bet you thought I would die, so there was no use for me anymore, beside making money of course. And you all could do all that in my absence so it was fitting. There was no need to even check on me, through a thirty second call."

"That's… that's not true, Dom…" Makayla stammered. Nervously, she ran a hand over the sides of her short blonde hair.

"Oh really?" Dom sat back in his paved seat and crossed his arms. "Are you going to tell me that the reason you are here is not to convince me that you are still on my side so I can renew the publishing contract?"

"Of course not! Why would I…?"

"You counted your eggs before they hatched, Makayla. Now that you see I am fine and well, without a doubt you realize that I most likely know you for what you are. You didn't think I will survive till this time so you never thought about the soon to expire contract."

Her hand flew to her chest and she gasped, "Okay, that is just preposterous, Dom! I am greatly offended! What do you take us for? Liars and schemers?"

Dominic scoffed and leaned forward in his seat.

"You do realize that the night of the accident, I found out about all the shady things you and Harrison had planned out, in my name, right?"

"That's…" She swallowed hard and he could see the intensity in her blue eyes as she struggled to pull herself together. "There is an explanation for that. You see…"

"You can save your breath, Makayla. Back then, I planned to sleep and make my decision the next day." He chuckled and shook his head, "I ended up sleeping, but for longer than I wanted. Isn't it funny?"

"Really? Only you would joke about your accident," Ana said with an eye roll.

"I…"

"I will not be renewing my publishing contract with HarriM Publishing, Makayla. It is a decision that was made even before you stepped in here. I apologize for wasting your time, but I was curious to see how far you would go with the lies and deceit. I have to admit that, it has been quite amusing."

Her nostrils flared and she formed a fist around the strap of her bag. She jumped to her feet.

"You are a frigging bastard, Dominic! Who on earth do you think you are?!"

"The contract ends today. We can put an end to this charade of a friendship along with it, don't you think?" Dominic smiled, tilting his head.

"With pleasure! It's been so hard having to stand you and your Mr. Goodie-two-shoes ways. Don't think you are so special because you choose not to do what the others are doing!"

"Lying, cheating, being corrupt? Yeah, I don't think I am special, Makayla. I am just trying to be a good person," he said with a shrug.

"Bastard!" She hissed and stormed off, her hig heeled shoes clicking on the floor as she slammed the door behind her, her mini cooper screaming its wheels as she sped off in the dark.

"So much for an amicable farewell," An amused Dominic said as he turned to his sister.

Ana chuckled, "I like that she got this furious."

"You do?"

"Uh huh. It shows how much it hurts that you turned them down and didn't fall for their tricks. It was her embarrassment and disappointment speaking in the end. Like they say, good riddance."

"Yeah..." Dominic said softly. He sighed and ran a hand through his hair tiredly.

His sister reached forward and squeezed his hand, "I am sorry, brother. I know you cared about them greatly. You still care about them and this hurts you."

"Yeah, but what I can say is I am glad I am alive to cut them off."

She smiled and nodded. "So, have you eaten today?"

"Yeah, I had a salad earlier."

Ana snorted, in an unsuccessful bid to hold back her laughter.

"Really? My pain is funny to you, huh?"

She grinned, "I apologize, big brother, it is just so funny hearing you say you had a salad. The old Dominic would have either had a protein bar or a glass of water, and be hard at work on his computer at this time." As he walks trough the big kitchen past the designer coffee machine.

He rolled his eyes, "Whatever."

"It is funny how the topic your mother has been lecturing you about for so long, a heart attack succeeded in convincing you to actually take it serious and start towing the right path. She should be grateful to it."

Dominic threw his head back and laughed, "Do not let your mother hear you say that. You are going to get a very long lecture."

"You don't have to tell me. Just last night, I joked about how your accident awoke her dormant detective genes, and she has it to thank. Let's just say, mom still has a perfect aim when making slippers fly."

Dominic chuckled and shook his head, "Ana!"

His sister shrugged and winked. Dominic's smile slipped and he said, "Does she still think my accident was intentional? She has not said anything to me about it again."

"Well, after that day in the hospital, I have found her deep in thought a few times and when I asked, she said someone is after your life."

"What?"

"Yeah, but she only said it when she was in a dazed state. I mean, every time, she jolted back to reality and did not seem to remember what she said."

"That's worrisome." Dominic sighed. "The past few months must have been really rough on mom. And on all of you. I am so sorry."

"Yes, but, thank you for coming back, rather than heading off to oblivion from there." His sister told him with a wink.

"Ha, ha, very funny," Dominic smiled. He sat back in his seat and tapped his chin, "Did the police say anything? What did the incident report say?"

"Hmm… I don't think the police ever investigated your accident. There was already a record of you calling emergency services because of your heart attack. There was likely no need for them to do so. Why? Do you believe what mom says? I mean, I do not think it is impossible, but it is normal to feel paranoid after what we all went through, right?"

"Right…" Dominic said slowly. He shook his head and said, "Besides, I cannot think of anyone who would want to do that to me. I know this is a cut-throat world, but I mostly keep to myself and… you know what? I am just overthinking it. Let's talk about something else."

"Sure. Now, that you have gotten rid of HarriM, what is your next step? Do you have a publishing company in mind?"

He shrugged, "I am talking a break from writing, you know that. You heard what the doctor said. I need to be careful with my decisions in the next months, and take it easy to avoid a repetition of what happened, and to improve the quality of my health."

"I know, but it must be really hard for you. I bet you have a million folders filled with ideas and plans…" He averted his gaze and his sister smiled knowingly. "I am right… look at your face, you cannot even deny it."

"Yeah, whatever. I just keep compiling them, all right? That does not mean I am going to do anything about it."

"Okay, I hear you. You better not, because I know the word 'rest' has been torn out of your dictionary. You better take it easy so we do not return to the hospital in an ambulance."

Dominic scoffed, "Like you would not be glad to see the doctor."

His sister's eyes widened, "Oh for crying out loud!"

"What? The chemistry between the two of you did not go unnoticed by anyone, I am just saying. And… guess what? He is single so I think you both can work quite well." Dominic winked.

"I am not going to sit here and listen to this. I will fix myself a meal, at least I know there is actually food in this house. We can thank your heart attack for that."

She jumped to her feet and speed walked to the kitchen.

"Hey, don't try to change the topic," Dominic hurried after her.

CHAPTER FOUR

GLASS WALLS, LUSH greenery through the glass walls, clear blue skies, that was all that surrounded him every day. Dominic sighed and backed away from the kitchen sink where he had been cleaning his coffee mug. He was bored, freaking bored out of his mind. He needed an escape. But how was he going to achieve that when he was always stuck in here?

Well, it was not like his doctor said he should coop himself up and never go out. So, why then was he inside? He frowned. It was because he never did have a social life, even before the accident. His entire life had been his work, so now that he could not write, he had nothing to do but stare into space all day.

"You need to do something new, you need to get yourself a hobby." Those had been his doctor's words during his last checkup. Dominic scoffed. It was easier said than done. He ran a hand through his head of full brown hair. His phone buzzed just then. Absentmindedly, he picked it up from the countertop. A smile spread across his face when he saw it was a picture from his sister. It was more gifts from his fans. His home address was private so they kept sending them to his mother's café, which was one of the few private information that they had been able to dig up about him.

His smile deepening, he scrolled through the pictures of the cards, feeling very grateful to his readers. Everyone was wishing he felt better soon and returned to the field.

"Me and you all," Dominic muttered. "Me and you all."

Dominic decided that it was time he actually started making concrete steps to improve his social life. He was not going to achieve anything by seating on his ass in his living room in his glass house. There had to be something out there he could do, something that would resonate with him.

He grabbed his car keys and headed out the door. The man pulled out of his driveway with no destination in mind. He was just looking for something that would call out to him. About thirty minutes of driving later, Dominic found himself pulling into an overcrowded parking lot in front of a mall. He sat behind the wheel for a few minutes longer, trying to make up his mind about alighting or not. The bored part of him finally won the struggle and he stepped out of the car.

Dominic made his way through a teeming crowd of people. At that moment, there was a part of him regretting not staying at home. The mall was just too rowdy for him. Nonetheless, it felt good to be out of the house for the first time in a long while. It was overwhelming, but it was definitely a brand-new experience for him. Not really having anything in mind, Dominic let himself be pushed forward by a crowd of people. Within seconds, he found himself standing in the cinema entrance hall.

"A movie is not such a bad idea," the man grinned. He joined the longest queue. Surely the movie had to be good if there were so many people who wanted to watch it. That was the rationale behind his decision.

Dominic felt something soft hit his back and he turned around in time to see a rubber ball bouncing off him, just as a little boy ran to it. A flustered man hurried after the boy, while a woman who was pushing a stroller with a younger child in it smiled apologetically as she said,

"I am so sorry about Tommy. He can be quite a handful, especially when we are outdoors."

"It is fine," Dominic nodded and turned to his front. He watched the young family as they joined the next queue which was clearly for a child-friendly movie judging from the fact that they were not the only family with children on it.

Dominic tilted his head as he watched the father gently raise the boy up to the sky, causing the kid to laugh heartily and say, "Do it again, dad, do it again."

His father did do it again and Dominic chuckled as he saw the little one in the stroller laugh cheekily. Warmth enveloped him and a thought ran through him, *Being able to make your child laugh like that must be so fulfilling. It must be amazing caring for your little one like that and knowing that you would do your all to be there for your child.*

Dominic was so lost in his thoughts as he looked at the family longingly that he did not realize it was his turn on the queue.

"How many tickets are you buying, sir? Hello?"

He turned back to the attendant who was looking at him inquisitively.

"How many tickets do you want to buy sir?"

"Uh…" Dominic looked around him, realizing for the first time that most of the people on the queue behind him and even the ones now seated were in groups of two or three, or more. It seemed like he was the only one that was actually alone. Sure, there was nothing wrong in watching a movie alone, but at that moment, he was feeling very lonely and watching a movie by himself was not something he wanted to do.

"Are you going to buy a ticket, sir?" the attendant asked again. The people behind him were already getting impatient.

"Sorry," Dominic said and he quickly stepped out of the queue, letting the trio behind him go ahead.

What is wrong with you, Dominic? He asked himself. He had never longed for company and had always been perfectly okay being with himself, and having just his mother, sisters and Angelica in his life, and the few friends he had. Even with his friends, he barely went out, preferring to have home meetings or dates, so he was not too far away from his computer and could get to work whenever a strike of inspiration occurred. But with Angelica, he had gone out a lot, to places she liked and wanted to go to. He felt a bitter taste in his mouth at the thought of Angelica. He had loved her so much and thought she was the right one for him.

They had met during a book signing event of an author he got along quite well with. They had hit it off right away, which was rare for someone like him who was very careful and observant of people.

Within months, they had started dating and he had been so sure she loved him as much as he loved her. For her, he had compromised a lot of times. And now that he thought about it, not once had she ever compromised for him. He had always been the one adjusting himself for her in the relationship. And he had never minded it. He had been in love with her and all he cared about was making her happy, being happy with her. But it was clear now to him that they had both had different priorities in the relationship.

Dominic shook his head and headed out of the cinema hall. There was no use beating himself about what was gone. Yes, he had lost Angelica but maybe he had never had her in the first place. Her actions after the accident showed that. It was true that the accident affected his lifestyle in so many ways, but another big truth was the fact that the accident revealed to him who the snakes were in his life. Of course, he would not wish to be in an accident again but this accident had been pretty eye-opening.

A smile spread across the man's face when he found himself staring at the entrance of a bookstore. Without hesitation, he went in. Dominic walked through the aisles, loving the smell of new books and feeling at home. He quirked a brow when he saw the books on the best seller aisle. Two of them were his. It was no wonder Harrison and Makayla had tried to take advantage of him and keep him signed with them. It was not because they cared but more about what they did not want to lose if he left them. They would be fine, he was sure of it. If there was one thing he knew, it was the fact that their company boasted a portfolio of great authors. So he was sure that even in his absence, they would be all right.

Dominic grabbed a few books that caught his attention and headed to the front desk to pay for them. Just as he was making his way out of the bookstore, he bumped into a woman.

"I am sorry," Dominic was quick to say.

She raised her head revealing a heart-shaped face framed with curly honey colored hair. Dominic froze and took a sharp intake of breath before he felt himself again.

"Are you okay?" she asked softly. She stared at him with large green eyes that rendered him speechless. All he could to do was nod, unable to open his mouth. "Okay."

She headed into the bookstore, leaving him to stare after her. Dominic was broken out of his daze by his ringing phone. The man rolled his eyes when he saw who was calling. Why was it so hard for her to get the message? He wondered. He has been ignoring Angelica's calls since he left the hospital, but she still kept calling. He had absolutely nothing to say to her, and he really did not want to see her. But it seemed like she was not going to understand anytime soon.

"What do you want, Angelica? Please make it quick." Dominic said as briefly as possible.

"Can we see each other?" her soft voice floated to him.

"No, we cannot. I have nothing to say to you, Angelica." he was quick to say.

"I miss you, Dom, so much…"

He sighed, and as calmly as he could, Dominic said, "That was not what you thought when I was in the hospital fighting for my life."

"Please, Dom, I have so much I need to say to you. Please, just meet me. And if after we see each other, and you listen to me, you still want nothing to do with me, then I won't bother you again."

"Fine, I will see you now," Dominic said tightly.

"Great! I will come to the house," the excitement was back in her voice.

"Don't bother, I will meet you at Rico's." He had no plans of letting her into his house, and there was no way she could even get in anymore, seeing how his passcode had been changed. He probably never would have thought about it but Ana had done it while he was in the hospital. And when he asked her why when he found out, she had replied, "To keep the pests out, of course. You never can tell what they are up to."

"Oh? But why do we have to meet in public. I think it will be better for us to meet where it is private and cozy, like your house, don't you think?" He heard the sultriness that she always infused in her voice whenever she wanted something. He could already picture her batting her eyelashes and twirling a strand of hair around her finger. Yep, indeed she had perfected the art of seduction, and he had constantly fallen for it.

"Yeah, that is not going to happen, Angelica. I will not be meeting you at my house, your house or anyone's house. If we cannot meet at Rico's, we have nothing whatsoever to talk about. Now, if you will excuse me."

"It's fine, fine, we can meet at Rico's. I will see you there in an hour?"

"Sure…" Dominic said slowly as he hung up. He stared at his phone thoughtfully as he made his way out of the mall. There was something about the call that did not sit right with him. Was it her desperation? Or her insistence that they meet in private? He had no clue what it was but he did not feel good about it. Maybe it was because he was a writer but there was something about her insistence that he found quite alarming.

Dominic speed dialed Ana as he got to his car.

"Hey, sis, I need you."

"What's wrong?" came his sister's alarmed voice.

"I am meeting Angelica and I cannot shake off this weird feeling in my gut."

His sister's exasperated sigh was her response, followed by, "Why on earth will you agree to meet her? Anyway, send us the location. Eva and I will be there. I don't trust that girl one bit. Who knows what she is up to now? Do not go in if we are not there. Do you understand? Don't meet her till we are with you."

"Yes, yes, I hear you." Dominic sighed. Sometimes he forgot who was the older sibling. "And oh, Ana?"

"Yes?"

"Bring them with you."

"With pleasure," his sister said excitedly.

CHAPTER FIVE

"WELL? SPILL IT. What is it you want to talk about?" Ana nudged Angelica waving her hand.

Angelica swallowed hard and looked from one sibling to the other. "Dom, when you said we could meet up, I didn't realize that you were coming with your family."

"Well, you didn't ask, did you?" Ana inserted.

"Ana…" Dominic threw her a look. She rolled her eyes and made a gesture of zipping her mouth. Dominic turned back to Angelica and said, "What would you like to say, Angelica? I think it is only fair my sisters are present as witnesses to whatever happens here. Do you not agree?"

"Witnesses?" she scoffed. "What exactly do you mean by that? We were in a relationship for three years and you still don't trust me. what then were we doing together?"

Dominic took a sip of his water and set the glass down. He smiled, crossed his hands and leaned back in his seat. "What is up with you all trying to gaslight me these days, in a bid to get your way?"

"Gaslight? Me…?" she gasped.

"You know, I find myself asking, is it that this has been going on for so long but I was too blinded to see it? Or is it that this just started, borne out of the desperation of you all? Which is it, ex-girlfriend?" he raised an eyebrow.

"You are not being fair to me, Dom. All I have ever done is love you, and here you are acting like I trapped you in some abusive relationship."

"And now you are just throwing words around," Dominic said, clearly amused. "You said you want to explain a few things to me. Well, go on, I am all ears. Or rather, we are all ears."

She breathed deeply and sat back in her seat. "I did not abandon you in the hospital, Dom, contrary to what you and your family think."

Ana opened her mouth to speak but Eva nudged her ribs, causing her mouth to clamp shut.

"Look, I was scared, all right? Put yourself in my shoes. The man I loved was fighting for his life. I was scared and I blamed myself for convincing you to go to the event. This was why I stayed away, I felt so guilty."

"And this prevented you from coming to check on me. You didn't even come once. You didn't even pick up your phone to call my family. You certainly did a great job staying away."

"I never stopped loving you, Dom. I am so sorry I let my guilt keep me away from you when you needed me the most. I just… I just could not forgive myself for putting you in that situation. I love you, Dom."

Dominic nodded slowly, "So, what about Jeep Smith?"

"What?" Her face crumpled in panic.

"You know who I am talking about, Angelica. Are you really going to deny that you and him have something together? It is all the tabloids were talking about for a long time, so I heard."

"Since when did you start reading those trash sites, Dom? Are you going to believe some nonsense over me, the woman you love? My love, Jeep and I are just friends. You know that. We went to the same high school and we have stayed in touch since then. Remember we even went for that cocktail party at his? Why would I possibly have anything to do with him when I have you, the one I love with all my heart?"

Dominic and his sisters stared at Angelica, shock written on their faces.

"This is absolutely amazing," Ana gasped.

"Like, I am shocked beyond belief. You are one damn good liar, Angelica. You know, you could totally become an actress. It seems it is your calling. You need to leave behind the world of a celebrity stylist and go become an actress. That is your calling not styling celebrities." Eva shook her head.

"Ana, I understand, but you, Eva? I cannot believe you would fall for all these lies that are being pandered. I expect that you would defend me and tell your brother the truth. I would expect this from Ana as she has never liked me, but not you."

"Wow, Ana has really always been the best judge of character. I need to listen to her more often," Eva uttered, still staring at Angelica in disbelief.

Angelica fumed as she turned to Dominic. "I will not sit here and listen to your sisters insult me. I thought you agreed to meet me so we can have a civil conversation, and iron out issues and we can get back together, but it is crystal clear to me that you have no interest in any of that. You literally brought your sisters to me, just so they can mock me. I will not stand for it. This is your last chance to save this relationship, Dominic."

"Ana?" Dominic stretched out his hand and his sister placed a large brown envelope in it. His sisters turned to Angelica as he opened the envelope. As he pulled out its contents, Dominic said, "You are right, indeed, Angelica. I would never believe trashy blog sites. But you should know me enough to know that I never speak weak words. I say what I mean and I never say anything without backing, so that I am not left with regrets. I am not perfect but I do try to live a good life."

Dominic slid four photographs across the table to lie perfectly before Angelica's eyes. Her hand flew over her mouth and she gasped. Her eyes flooded with tears and she looked up.

"Dom, Dom, I can explain. I…"

"You both just happened to be naked in bed together because it was really hot?" Dominic smiled. He stood up and dusted nonexistent lint off his coat. "It took two days for a private investigator to get me this proof."

"It's not what you think. Look, it was just one time and…"

"In case you didn't get it before, I will spell it loud and clear to you. This relationship is over, Angelica. We are done. And you should probably know that I know that your affair with Jeep has been on for about two years. I do have a very good PI."

"Dom, please…" she tried to grab his hand but he pulled away.

"You should have known when I didn't call you that your jig was up. Being met with pictures of you across blogs was not even hurtful, Angelica. I was not bothered by any of it. What bothered me was the fact that you were absent from my side and had no care in the world, whether I survived or not, and that prompted me to get a PI to find out what really is going on with my so-called girlfriend."

"Tsk, tsk, tsk, the perfect girlfriend who flew to California for work, but really was just on a trip with her lover," Ana hissed. "You really are so shameless, Angelica."

"Dom, this isn't...."

"It feels like I have more reasons to thank this crazy accident for happening. In its aftermath, I have certainly been able to separate the wheat from the chaff in my life. Anyway, you can keep the pictures. I won't be needing them."

"Toodles," Ana waved at Angelica as the siblings headed out of the restaurant. Angelica called out to him, but he ignored her, not sparing a second look.

"You always see the best in people," Ana was saying to Eva as the siblings settled into their favorite booth at their mother's café.

"And you always see the worst in them," Eva said pointedly.

Ana shook her head, "No, that is not true. I like to think I see the part that they are trying so hard to hide. I see through them and see them for what they really are, liars and scammers. Now, if everyone would just listen to me, but some people," she looked pointedly at their brother who was focused on what he was reading in his phone, "Would rather prefer to learn the hard way."

"And I take it that I am one of the people you are referring to?" Dominic quirked a brow.

"Well, if the shoe fits.." she trailed off.

"Wear it," Eva finished.

"Very funny," he shook his head and turned back to his phone.

"Ooh… what are you so focused on?" Ana tried to look over his shoulder, but even seated, he was still much taller compared to her five feet, six inches height. "Oh my, are you already searching for a date on Tinder?"

"Of course not. Why would your brother need to scour Tinder for a date? Do you realize that he is considered a hot catch?" a voice asked from behind the siblings.

The three of them groaned without turning around. They already knew who it was. The plump woman with bright pink lips plopped into the seat beside Dominic and wagged a brow, "Dom! Your mother says you and Angelica have broken up."

"You seem very excited about that, Miss Potts," Ana chuckled.

"Of course I am. How many times have I told you all that I know the perfect person for Dominic? She is beautiful, smart and such a good person, unlike that Angelica. You know, I never liked her and no one ever listened to me."

"No one ever listened to you, Miss Potts, because you are a biased party. You keep going on and on about this niece of yours," Eva pointed out.

"That is because you never listen. I have no idea what on earth is wrong with her and Dominic. I have lost count of the number of times I have told her about this handsome, smart man I want her to meet. But she keeps turning him down. He is handsome and smart, what more does she want? She is beautiful and smart, what more does he want?"

"She seems like a really smart one, seeing how she is not letting you influence her decisions, nor is she falling for the 'handsome' and 'smart' tag, Miss Potts," Dominic told her absentmindedly. "I wonder if it is because she does not trust your opinion? Very interesting. It begs the question, whether I can trust your opinion as well."

"Ever the smart aleck and smart mouth, I see…" Miss Potts hmphed. "I don't know why I even keep trying to help you when you clearly do not appreciate my help.

"I wonder the same thing, myself, Miss Potts, oh I wonder," came Dominic's reply.

The woman gasped and stormed off, most likely to find their mother and recant in a very dramatic way how her children had been extremely rude to her.

"Okay, what exactly are you up to? Now, I want to know," Eva leaned forward. "You are always so polite to Miss Potts but you did not so much as spare her a glance. Clearly, there is something very interesting in that phone of yours that has captivated your attention. Come on, brother. Are you really going to keep it from us?"

"It is not a big deal," Dominic said with a shrug. "I just came across an ad and it has led me to some pretty interesting information. It turns out that this is just what I might have been looking for. I am trying not to be too excited until I find something that actually captures my attention."

"Ooh… don't tell me you are really on Tinder, brother," Ana gasped. "Okay, you should know that I cannot just judge people through their pictures. I actually have to physically meet them before I can decide if they are good for you. Although, technically, there are a few times I am still able to tell the character of someone by looking at their pictures. Which means, I can still help you and…"

"You talk way too much," Dominic rolled his eyes, "Don't be ridiculous. I just got out of a relationship. I am not looking to jump into another."

As soon as he said the words, the face of a certain curly haired woman popped into his head, causing him to clear his throat and shake his head. It was only a few hours ago that he bumped into her, so why did it feel like it was a long time ago. Maybe it was because a lot of things had happened between now and then, starting with the fact that he had officially ended things with Angelica.

"Well, if it is not Tinder or any other dating site, what is it? Are you not going to show it to us?" Eva asked, stretching a hand out for his phone.

"It really is no big deal, all right? And Ana, this is especially for you. I do not need you running off to Dr. Perry to tell him that I have resumed working and stressing myself, because this is nothing like that. This is actually me finding a way to actually take it easy," Dominic said to his sister as he placed the phone on the table.

"Hey! What is that supposed to mean? Why do you keep linking me with the good doctor?"

"Maybe because of the sparks that always flies when both of you see each other?" Eva chuckled as she picked up the phone.

"Thank you very much. I am not the only one who sees it. Remember my checkup last week when you went with me, not Ana? He actually could not prevent himself from asking about Ana. I tell you, there is something there," Dominic grinned.

"Worry about your love life, first," Ana pouted. She leaned toward the phone and quirked a brow. "This is a freelancing website."

"I know, Captain Obvious."

"What does this have to do with you? And why are you so excited about it? I believe that is the question that Ana wanted to ask," Eva supplied.

"Exactly," Ana nodded.

Dominic shrugged, "I thought it would be obvious."

They continued to stare at him blankly. He rolled his eyes and said, "So you know how I have all these ideas? They keep flowing, and all I can do is take it easy and record them with the hopes of working on them after my hiatus."

"Uh huh." His sisters nodded, looking at him expectantly.

"I do not know if you already know where I am heading to and you are just teasing me, or if you are genuinely clueless about the direction I am going in.."

"Anytime today would be nice, brother," Ana told him.

He rolled his eyes and said, "Fine. I want to hire a ghostwriter."

"A ghostwriter? Like a ghost, ghost?" Ana asked.

"Really?" Dominic groaned, causing his sisters to laugh.

"We get it, all right? We figured it out at the start of your explanation, but that does not stop us from teasing you because it is loads of fun," Eva grinned.

"Whatever," he tried to retrieve his phone but his sisters kept scrolling through, refusing him access.

"But are you sure about this? You have all these ideas in your head, are you sure this person will be able to portray the work the way you want?"

He shrugged, "That is what I will just have to see, right? How this site works is, you see samples of the works of the ghostwriter and you make a decision. Once I make a decision, I can reach out to the ghostwriter and provide my plot or story idea."

"And this person develops it and writes the story," Ana completed.

"Exactly," he said with a nod.

"Hmm… it does not seem bad. Seems like a pretty solid arrangement," Eva chipped in.

"Yes, but there has to be a certain level of trust between the two parties involved. On the part of the buyer, trust that the writer will deliver the work when due, and will also not claim ownership of the work. And on the part of the writer, trust that the buyer will not run off and will actually do the right thing and pay for the finished story, the product," Ana mused.

"That is very correct," Dominic said. "Ghostwriting is not new and is just like every other service being rendered. It works out well, as long as all parties are good, honest and responsible. This is the kind of relationship I hope to build with a ghostwriter I find, a respectful and trusting one."

"So you have to choose carefully," said Eva.

"Uh huh," Dominic agreed as he finally retrieved his phone from his sisters.

"We can help you choose. What do you think?" Ana clasped her hands together and batted her eyelashes.

"No, thank you. I am pretty sure I can handle this. But thank you so much for offering to take the time out of your busy schedule to help me make this life changing choice," he teased her.

"Really? Really? I am offering to help you here and you are being so ungrateful," she chuckled. "Weren't you all just talking about how I am a good judge of character like a few minutes ago?"

"Oh, no one is disputing that fact, my dear sister, but that does not mean that your help will always be accepted when offered. If you want to help, would you be a dear and help me decide on what to eat? Thank you."

"You are awfully annoying," Ana gasped. He chuckled as she nonetheless reached for the menu.

Dominic turned his attention back to his phone, scrolling through the various profiles that kept popping up. None called out to him yet. The funny thing was that he had no idea what he was searching for but he knew he would know when he found it.

His thumb suddenly froze over a profile. The display picture was a picture of one of his favorite books when he was younger, Pippi Longstocking. He chuckled and opened the profile. Dominic nodded slowly as his eyes scanned the writer's profile. The bio said that it was a woman.

Lover of everything sweet, and writer of deep stories that transcends time.

Of everything that was written in the bio, those were the words that popped out to him. They seemed awfully familiar, like words he had heard a lot in the past but he could not place it. His memory was failing him and he could not recall why those words were so familiar.

He shook his head. Whatever it was, it was not important. He had found the one. He could feel it in his gut. He had found what he was looking for, without realizing that it was what he had been searching for. She was the one.

"Did you hear what I said, Dom?" his sister asked him.

"Huh?" Dominic asked, not looking away from his phone.

"I was asking if you want grapes or blueberry."

"Anyone is fine," Dominic replied as without another moment's hesitation, he sent a message to the ghostwriter.

Hello, he sent.

CHAPTER SIX

THE STORY IS amazing. You are truly an incredible writer. I do not think I could have done it better myself. If anything, you definitely portrayed the story just how I would have done it. I want to do more work with you, if you are okay with that, of course. I have sent payment for the first job with a bonus which I believe is very deserving. Please let me know what you think of this plot I am attaching. If you like it and it is something you can do, we can go ahead and open a new contract.

Dominic sat back in his chair and turned to the manuscript he had printed out. He was very excited. The ghostwriter had certainly outdone herself and he was more than convinced that he wanted to work with her again.

The sound of an incoming message pulled him back to his computer screen. It was from the ghostwriter and her message was brief and straight to the point as it always was. It read, *Okay. I will get started on it. If I have any questions, I will let you know.*

Dominic smiled and closed his laptop. He had not really been expecting much from her but that. He had come to realize that her brief responses did not mean annoyance. He was indeed enjoying the work relationship and hoped that it would continue being a good one. Feeling fulfilled, he turned in for the night.

Dominic woke up in the middle of the night in cold sweats. He run his fingers through his damp hair, as he struggled to calm himself. He had had a nightmare, but he could not remember it. All he knew was that it had been so bad and had forced him to jolt awake. He groaned in fatigue. This was not the first time it was happening. It was already two months since he left the hospital and if memory served him well, the nightmares and cold sweats had started after he returned from the hospital. He did not have them every night but he did have them some nights. Unfortunately, tonight was one of such nights.

Dominic pushed off the bed and slipped his feet into his slippers. He knew from experience that he was not going to get any more sleep tonight. There was no point trying to force himself as it would be a lost mission even before it started.

Dominic padded across the floor and made his way to the first floor where he found his way to the kitchen. He filled a glass with cold water and took an appreciative sip. The glowing hands of the clock told him that it was a little past one pm.

You asleep? He shot a message at his sisters. No response.

Why are you still awake, old man? Will your doctor be pleased to see this? I was certainly not pleased to see the notification that you are online. A message popped into his phone.

Dominic chuckled and sent a message to his friend in response, *You are one to talk. You aren't any older than I am.*

Ha! I didn't just have a heart attack, so there is that, the new message came in, causing Dominic to laugh hard. For a moment, he temporarily forgot about his problem.

But seriously, why are you still awake, man? I thought you were trying to take it easy. That includes sleeping early and well enough, Dom.

Dominic smiled softly. Wesley had moved into serious mode quite quickly.

I just had a hard time sleeping, so I decided to take a break from it. Dominic sent to Wesley.

His response came quickly, *Are you having sleep problems? When did they start? You need to tell your doctor, man. This is not something you should trifle with. What if it is a side effect of the accident? You cannot sit on this, man!*

Dominic could literally hear his friend screaming from his message.

Yes, yes, I will, man. I plan to let him know what is going in our next appointment. Now, can you please stop mothering me?

Whatever. You better take care of yourself, man. Don't go having another heart attack. And you should be trying to sleep right, else, I will let your mother know about this. I am not joking.

Dominic chuckled. Oh he knew all too well that his friend was not joking. He was vaguely reminded of a time back in college when he had had been on a writing marathon, refusing to break to eat or sleep. The ideas had kept coming and he did not want to stop. His priorities had certainly been skewed for a really long time, Dominic shook his head. He smiled as he remembered how after two days, his friend and roommate, Wesley had put a call through to his mother and she had stormed over to the campus with more than a lecture for him. His smile slipped when he thought about how contrasting and different Wesley's friendship was to Harrison's and Makayla's. He could actually not remember a time when they had actually been concerned about his health. Instead, they had encouraged him to work even harder. Of course working hard was not a bad thing, but when it was at the detriment of one's health, then it was time to adjust one's priorities and make necessary amendments.

Thanks man. I will get some sleep soon. Good night. Dominic sent back.

Good night, man. I will be in New York in a few weeks. We should catch up. Now, go get some sleep, man. Alex just asked who I am chatting with, while still sleeping. I don't know how the woman does it. Anyway, she has sleepily told me to wish you a great day.

Dominic smiled at his friend's response and set his phone on the table. At that moment, he could vividly remember Wesley's scream when he spoke with him after he woke up from the coma. By midnight, Wesley was in New York to see him with his own eyes and confirm that he was indeed alive. He had been blessed with a few good friends in his life, and Dominic knew that Wesley was one of them. There was a time that he had thought Harrison was one, but he had been wrong. Maybe it was because he had been too blind to see, or maybe he had just been a good pretender. He really could not tell. What he was sure of was that Harrison out of his life was good riddance.

A few weeks later, Dominic opened his front door and laughed to see Wesley on his front stoop. Wesley stretched his hands out and said,

"I told you I would be in your city soon."

"That you did, that you did. Come on in, man. Alex not with you?" Dominic asked as he closed the door behind his friend.

"'Nah, she has a big case she is working on."

"She is the police chief right? That is awesome." Dominic handed his friend a glass of freshly squeezed juice which he accepted gratefully.

"Oh yes, it is." Wesley smiled proudly.

"So, is she usually one of your sources?"

Wesley laughed. "She has served as a consultant for me, yes. That is all I am going to say."

"Well, I will come calling the next time I am writing a thriller," Dominic grinned. He took a sip of his juice and set the glass on the table.

"That is very much okay. Alex thoroughly enjoys being a consultant and sharing her knowledge. It is why she continues teaching at the police academy, even though she does not have to."

"And you are thoroughly in love with your wife. Your eyes glint so much when you talk about her. I am really happy for you, man."

"Thanks, Dom. I am lucky to have her. So… about you and Angelica… come on, drop that expression, man. You told me you would tell me all that happened when we see each other physically. I am curious to know what exactly transpired. She seemed quite… clingy."

"I would have kicked you out if you used the word 'lovey-dovey'," Dominic grinned, causing Wesley to laugh. "Oh yes, because it would be an obvious lie. I mean, she did not create the best first impression. I have a feeling that Alex is as eager to hear this story as much as you are, right?"

"Can I plead the fifth?" Wesley grinned.

Dominic chuckled and shrugged, "What can I say, man? She had been cheating on me for years, and the fact that I was unconscious in a hospital did not stop her. it only intensified her efforts, probably because she thought I would not make it. You know, not once did she check on me when I was in the hospital."

"Damn, that is cold."

"Uh huh. It is what it is. She did try to scheme her way back but I have no plans of letting her back into my life. She finally got the message when I showed her the pictures. What else could she say when she was caught red-handed and had been confronted with the evidence?"

"I am very sorry, man. You are a good person and you did not deserve to get entangled with someone like her." Wesley patted his back.

"Yeah. I was stupid and naïve, and blind if I may say. Our breakup is one of the many things I can thank the accident for, I guess. I am trying to move on from all that and start afresh, which means having nothing to do with her."

"You will meet a good person soon, my friend. You deserve to be with someone who is deserving of your kindness and your kind heart."

"That means a lot. Thank you, man." Dominic smiled at his friend. He tapped his chin as he said, "You know, I just realized that you are dressed too formally to visit me."

Wesley grinned, "Always astute, I see. I have a lunch meeting with some of my publisher buddies and authors they just signed on later today, so I have to look quite sharp."

"That sounds nice. It should be fun," Dominic said thoughtfully.

"I guess so," Wesley agreed with a nod. "Why is that expression on your face?"

"Can I come with?"

"What?"

"Can I tag along? I have come to realize in recent times that I had a very nonexistent social life besides my family and Angelica. Removing them from the equation, all I had was work. I am trying to be more social and mingle more, with a circle of likeminded people, of course. I think your lunch would be a good circle."

"Yeah... sure, they are all great guys, but..."

"But?"

Wesley sighed and said, "Right next door to ours is a luncheon being held by Charles and co, you know their entire sect. I do not know if you are comfortable with the thought of bumping into them. They have a way of ruining your mood, you know."

Dominic frowned, "I thought it was only me that felt that way when I see them. You know what? Sure, I will still come along. I can be civil to them, as long as they are civil of course. Let's do this."

Wesley quirked a brow, "What is the major reason you really want to come out with me?"

Dominic chuckled, "You know me too well. Well, aside these many reasons I have mentioned, there is a major one. I am trying not to think about something that I am looking forward to. I am expecting it anytime soon, but I do not want to think about it. You know how the saying goes, 'a watched pot never boils'. Thinking about it will do me no good so I need the distraction, so my dear friend, you picked the perfect day to come see me."

"All right then! Speak no more, my friend. Let's go have lunch!" Wesley cheered.

Wesley who was walking in front of Dominic suddenly groaned and froze in his tracks.

"What…?" Dominic was asking when he saw what his friend had seen.

"Well, well, well, Dominic Gray! Great to see you moving around, alive and well. You know, a lot of people said you would die, but me, I said there is no way that is going to happen because Dominic is very stubborn. He is like that weed that refuses to die, like hydra, you cut off a head and he rises stronger. They did not believe me but yet, here you are," Charles scoffed.

"Hello Charles," Dominic told him quietly.

"Is it not a pleasure to see me? You know, the only thing that bothered me about your accident is why you had to sleep. I mean, what was the point of sleeping for a few months if you were just going to wake up at the end of the day? Now, if you were going to die later, then by all means, the coma was necessary. I bet you must have found it bothersome, right?"

Wesley was about to say something but Dominic placed a calming hand on his friend's shoulder. To Charles, he said, "Nah, not really. It was a good sleep as it was an opportunity to find out more about the snakes who have been creeping around me. I mean, I know it is easy for you to live with snakes as you are one yourself, but for me, I am glad for the opportunity I got to weed them all out."

"Snake… me…" Charles' nostrils flared. He turned to the men who had been flanking him quietly and said, "The boys must be waiting for us. Let's go. Have a good lunch, Dom. I hope you won't choke on it. I would hate to see you go to the hospital in an ambulance twice in a year."

"Thank you for the fake show of concern. It looks quite flattering on you," Dominic nodded at him.

Fuming, Charles stormed away. Wesley chuckled and said to his friend, "Why does he always look angry after a conversation with you? I noticed the night of your accident too."

Dominic shrugged, "Maybe it is because he always comes in guns blazing and I am never bothered by it. I always tell him how it is, and he does not like it. Whatever. It really is none of my business. Come on, I am starving."

Dominic already knew everyone in the room, although not closely, but by virtue of the fact that they were all in the same industry and had run into each other once or twice. There was no need for introductions. A little while later, Dominic found that he was able to relax and enjoy his meal. He had been right to come along. This was indeed a good setting, filled with likeminded people.

As he took a sip of his juice, Dominic rubbed the back of his neck with his hand. The hairs were standing, and he had a niggling feeling that he was being watched. Dominic turned around but he could see nothing. The restaurant was a Korean restaurant and there were several private rooms. He was seated with his back to the wall so there was no one there. Why could he not shake off the feeling then? He wondered.

Dominic was seated across the doors and just then, they opened. He was surprised when an author he was familiar with from HarriM walked in.

"So sorry I am late," he apologized as he settled down next to Dominic.

"Oh it's okay," the others waved away his apology.

"Mr. Gray!" The man's face broke into a brilliant smile and he grabbed Dominic's hand. "It is so good to see you. It has been quite a while. I was really worried about you. I was so glad to learn you pulled through."

"Thank you, Rick, I saw your card."

Rick's eyes widened, "How is that possible? I heard you were receiving cards every week."

Dominic smiled, "Of course I read them all. I am grateful to you all and grateful for all your kind wishes, and for your prayers."

"That is nothing compared to all you do, Mr. Gray. You deserve goodness in your life because you are a good person too. I remember when I first joined HarriM, scared out of my wits. You pulled me aside and told me that I had so much talent and should have more confidence in myself. And you never failed to praise me at the few events we managed to drag you to."

Dominic smiled as nostalgia washed over him. That was about eight years ago. Those had indeed been good times.

"You did it all by yourself, you all did."

"With support from you, of course."

"I am happy you are doing very well, and I am very proud of you, which brings me to something I am confused about. Did you leave HarriM? All the authors here are recently signed to…" he trailed off.

"I am not the only one who left, Mr. Gray. After you left, it was a waterfall. I would say your exit was like the switching on of the tap."

"I don't understand. I thought you all loved it at HarriM."

"In the early days, yes, but all of that was lost a long time ago. Most of us stayed because of you, your mentorship and fear of the unknown. But with your exit and our discovery of all the bosses were up to, it made us realize that we were not being fair to ourselves staying there. We left in a horde."

"That is a shame to hear. I thought HarriM would be able to keep moving. I did not realize how bad things were on the inside. I am very sorry to you all, and I am glad you have found a place you fit in. I hope the same for the others."

Rick smiled appreciatively, "Thank you, Mr. Gray. Some of the other are still searching while some of us have found our new place, but the one thing that is missing from all our lives is regret. We do not regret leaving when we did."

"I am glad to hear that," Dominic smiled, "And I beg you, please stop calling me Mr. Gray. Dominic or Dom is just fine. You got that?"

Rick made to protest but the friendly, but stern look on Dominic's face caused him to smile and nod as he said, "Yes, Dominic. That sounds so weird."

Dominic chuckled, "You will get used to it in no time."

The lunch went on and occasionally, Dominic carried on a conversation with someone. But at the back of his mind was that feeling of being watched. By the time they were heading to the car, Dominic was more than glad to return home. He had appreciated the company of everyone he met, of course. But he still could not wait to get home.

"Sorry," a man said as he bumped into him just as they were leaving the restaurant. The man lowered his head and hurried off before Dominic could catch a better glimpse of his face. Dominic's eyes followed the back of the man's head, watching the streaks of golden yellow in his hair till his head disappeared around the corner.

"Hey, Dom, you good, man? Why are you just standing there?" Wesley tapped Dominic's shoulder.

Dominic shook his head, then looked back in the direction the man went. "I… I just feel like I am forgetting something, and there is something very familiar about that man."

"What man?" Wesley asked.

"Did you not see him? He bumped into me seconds ago."

"Uh… no. I was on a call with Alex though. Wait, check if your wallet is still on you. Could he be a pickpocket? That is what they do. They fake bump into you and use that opportunity to steal something. Is your watch missing? What of your phone?"

"You really are the husband of a police chief. All is intact, let's go," Dominic headed out before his friend could ask if his legs were missing too.

"But you said there was something familiar about this man, and you feel like you are forgetting something," Wesley reminded him when he caught up with him.

Dominic shrugged, "I feel a lot of things, all right? All through lunch, I felt like someone was watching me."

The man rubbed the back of his neck and sighed, "I still feel like I am being watched. It is not a good feeling."

"That is troubling."

Dominic shook his head, "It might just be sleep deprivation. I told you about the nightmares, right? I am not sleeping as well as I should and it is probably making me overthink during the day."

"I don't know about that, man. I have learned a lot from Alex and one of them is to know that you do not just ignore a gut feeling. If you feel something is wrong, maybe it is because something is wrong."

"Or maybe I am just being paranoid? Maybe this is just an aftereffect of all the drugs pumped into my system? The therapy? Man, there are a million and one reasons for this. I do not want to overthink it. Please, don't be like my mom. Let's go."

"Your mom?" Wesley quirked a brow. "What does your mom have to do with this? What did she say when you told her?"

"I did not tell her but because of something that happened, she was going on about people being after my life. Don't bother about any of it, man. Forget it."

"After your life? Come on, man. Is this not something you need to worry about?"

"No, all right? Look man, it is nothing. Do not overthink it. Come on, let's go. Come on, Wesley."

"Fine, fine, but I do not think this is something you should ignore, man, no matter how paranoid you think your mother is being," Wesley started to say as they entered the car.

That night found Dominic in front of his computer, refreshing his computer page every minute that passed. He was eagerly waiting for the new story from his ghostwriter. Gone were the worries he had felt earlier in the day and the niggling sensation.

Now that he was back in the safe haven of his home, he was reminded of the story and the reason he had craved the distraction earlier in the day in the first place.

The dinging sound that his computer always made when he received a message caused him to jump in his seat. A smile spread across Dominic's face as he opened the message from his ghostwriter. There it was, *Darling's Revenge.*

CHAPTER SEVEN

WHAT DO YOU *think about the accident happening at the construction site instead of close to the hospital?* Dominic smiled as he sent off the message.

About a minute later, a message came in, *Yes I agree with that. It definitely builds up the suspense at that scene. Let us work with that approach. Also, don't you think Amelia is coming off just too strong?*

I agree. I say we kill her off and wrap up her arc in the tenth chapter. Dominic replied.

Exactly what I was thinking. A smiling emoji was attached to the message from the ghostwriter.

Dominic grinned and replied with a thumbs up.

"Have you gotten yourself a girlfriend? Those are a whole lot of messages."

Dominic was startled by the voice that came from just beside his shoulder and he jumped up. His sister's laughter was the next thing he heard.

"Jeez, Ana, do you want to give me another heart attack? How can you creep up on me like that?"

"No, don't you dare say that," a giggling Ana managed to say. "I called out to you when I let myself into the house and even as I approached the kitchen but it is clear that you are lost in your own world and you were ignorant of my presence."

"I do not know what you are talking about." Dominic argued as he settled back into the stool.

"Right... Of course you do not. It's not like I did not see you grinning from ear to ear while you typed away on your phone. So, who is the lucky girl?"

"There is no lucky girl," Dominic was quick to say.

"So are you trying to say that my ears and my eyes were deceiving me? I clearly saw you laughing and typing away on your phone. Why then if it's not about a girl?"

Dominic rolled with his eyes and waved his phone in front of his sister's face as he said, "I was just having a conversation with my ghostwriter. Can you see? Not everybody is in a flirtatious relationship like you are with the dear doctor, you know."

"Okay, you should not try to turn this around and make it about me. I was just surprised as you looked like you were about to enter your phone and hug the person on the other end."

"Oh would you stop being so ridiculous?"

He made to collect his phone but his sister sidestepped him and continued scrolling through it.

"Wow, you and her have been communicating quite frequently. I do not blame myself for thinking you were talking to your girlfriend because this correspondence between you both, it is a lot. It is so friendly and chatty and wow... interesting."

He rolled his eyes and reached for his phone, "Stop being ridiculous. Can I please have my phone back?"

"How am I being ridiculous? From what I can see, you both obviously chat every single day. Sure right now, it is about work but I can already see some pleasantries sprinkled in here and there. Ooh... I see here that she told you she used to be a reporter and you told her you have two sisters. Interesting... it is becoming more personal as the days go by, huh? Who knows what this might evolve into some day?"

He sighed and finally retrieved his phone from her, "It is a good and warm friendship, dear Ana. Not all friendships will evolve into what you and the good doctor clearly want to happen, but are too shy to admit."

"Wow, wow," Ana gasped. "You are just on a roll today, I see."

He chuckled and said, "I am just being honest, dear sister. I think I can actually call my ghostwriter a friend now. We have a really good relationship. There is something very familiar about it, you know. It is comforting."

"Comforting? You rarely find strangers comforting," Ana quirked a brow.

"I know, right? That is what makes it so different this time. I mean, it is funny how we have never met but I feel very much myself with her. Chatting with her whenever I wake up in the middle of the night has certainly helped me a lot."

His sister's eyes narrowed at him, "What do you mean by that? Why are you waking up in the middle of the night, Dom?"

"Uh… what?" Dominic asked quickly. Oops, he had just shot himself in the foot. He had refused to tell his mother and sisters about the nightmares to prevent them from worrying and for a moment there, he had been so excited and he had forgotten. The only person who knew about the nightmares was Wesley, before now, that is.

"You heard my question, Dom. What is going on? What are you hiding?"

"Nothing, all right? I just have nightmares occasionally and they keep me up at night, sometimes." He tried to leave the kitchen but his sister blocked his path with her smaller frame.

She crossed her arms as she asked, "How often is 'occasionally', Dom?"

He shut his eyes and said, "Three, four times a week?"

She gasped, "You mean to tell me that you are losing sleep that many times, and you told us nothing about this? Why? What could be the reason? Have you told your doctor about this?"

Dominic shrugged, "I plan to tell him today, sister. Look, I am pretty sure that there is nothing to worry about. It is probably a result of the accident, all right? The trauma or something."

"What do you keep dreaming about though?"

Dominic sighed, "Sadly, I cannot even answer that question. I only remember that I am running. That is all I can recall when I wake up. And I am always in cold sweats. It is like I end up sweating in reality while I run in my dream."

He chuckled and his sister gave him a pointed and concerned look, "That is not funny, Dom. This is very worrisome."

"It is not. Look, I am sure I will be fine, okay? I did not tell you this so you can worry. Frankly, I had no plan of telling you if it had not slipped."

"You are annoyingly stubborn," she frowned at him.

"And I love you too," Dominic winked at his sister.

"You have to tell Dr. Perry about this, all right? Let's see what he says," she said sternly.

"And you won't tell…?" he wagged a brow.

She sighed and told him, "For the time being, I will not tell mom and Eva, but I cannot promise you how long I will keep it to myself. Now can you go get ready? We have your appointment, remember?"

"Fair enough," he nodded slowly. As he backed away from the kitchen, he grinned and said, "You know, I still do not understand why you all are still taking me to the doctor's office. I am not a baby, you know. I can manage on my own."

"We are going to be late if you plan to argue with me right now," his sister reminded him.

He raised his hands in surrender. "Fine, fine, I am going, baby sister."

Seeing the worry on her face, Dominic retraced his footsteps, planted a kiss on her cheek and hurried out before she could protest. Her laughter followed him out.

Dominic remained seated in the passenger's seat even after his sister alighted the car. He could feel it again, that niggling feeling of being watched. Ever since the lunch with Wesley and the other guys, this feeling had become a frequent company whenever he was outside. He could never shake off the thought that he was being watched. At first, he had chalked it up to paranoia, but now he was really not so sure anymore. What was real and what was not?

"Dom, are you not coming down?" his sister called. She waved at him from where she stood a few feet away.

Dominic swallowed hard and came down from the car. His eyes darted around as they always did whenever he was outside his home. Ana hurried to him and locked her arms with his. Before he could say anything else, she pulled him toward the entrance of the hospital, saying, "We have just five minutes left till our appointment. I really don't want to be late."

"Yeah… yeah…" Dominic managed to say as he let her pull him along. He stole one more glance at his surroundings before he was pulled into the building. After a series of routine tests, they were led to the office to wait for their turn to see the doctor.

Sometime later, they were ushered into Dr. Perry's office and the doctor jumped to his feet as soon as he saw them. He rushed forward, a soft smile on his face and nodded at Dominic as he said,

"Hello Mr. Gray." He immediately turned to Ana, "Hello, Miss Gray. You came today."

"Oh yes, I was free to come with Dom."

"It's great that you could come with him today," Dr. Perry said, his eyes focused on Ana.

"Oh yeah… I'm… uh… glad I was free to come with him." Ana said slowly, a smile playing on her lips. She pointed at his hair, "Uh… did you do something to your hair? A haircut?"

Dominic covered his mouth to hide his smile. He was trying really hard to hide his amusement. How on earth had his sister noticed the difference in the doctor's hair when even him that spent longer time with him had not even noticed? He grinned. He had a story to tell the others and after today, never again would they let her deny what was brewing between her and the doctor. Well, her and the good doctor were still denying to themselves, that was for sure.

"Oh… you noticed," Dr. Perry's brown eyes twinkled with delight as he touched his hazelnut brown hair. "I had a few days off… last week… so… I… uh…. got a haircut. Do you like it?"

"Yeah… I do. I mean, not that I had an issue with your previous haircut, you still looked good with it. I mean… uh… I just mean you look great now too," Ana blurted.

Oh, how much I long to record this conversation, Dominic thought, holding back his grin.

A blush spread across the doctor's cheeks as he said, "You look beautiful as always… and it's great to see you…"

"Would you like me to go out and give you both some alone time?" An amused Dominic finally asked, looking from his sister to the doctor.

The pair of them looked at him in surprise. It was obvious to Dominic that they had forgotten about his presence and he snorted in a desperate bid to hold back his laughter.

His sister rolled her eyes and backed away, "Don't be ridiculous. I will be outside. Just holla if you need me."

"Are you sure I will be the one who needs you?" Dominic chuckled. He was staring at the doctor whose eyes were fixated on his sister.

"Dom! Stop it!" she shout whispered. To the doctor, she smiled softly, "I am sorry about my brother's childish antics."

"Uh… it's okay…" the doctor stammered.

"I think you smiling like that will end up giving the good doctor a heart attack," Dominic whispered to his sister, but loudly enough that Dr. Perry could hear. The doctor smiled shyly and averted his gaze.

"I hate you right now," Ana glared at her brother as she made her way to the door. "You better tell him what we discussed earlier."

"Uh… what is that? Is something wrong?" the doctor looked between both of them.

"Dom is in the best place to explain everything. Bye." She hurried out, but not before Dominic noticed the blush that was already spreading across her cheeks.

He chuckled and turned to the doctor. It was cute and sweet that his sister had finally found someone that she actually liked and so surprising, how she got tongue tied too! That was the telltale sign that had made all of them realize that she liked the doctor, because Anastasia Gray was always a warrior and could never clamp up! Her being the reverse while talking to the doctor told Dominic and the other women in his life all they needed to know.

"May I sit now, Dr. Perry?" an amused Dominic asked.

"Sure, please. May I know what is wrong? What is Miss Gray talking about?"

Dominic's smile slipped and he became serious as he said, "Just persistent nightmares."

"Nightmares? How long has this been going on?"

"Since I left the hospital… don't look at me like that, doc. I did not see it as anything important because it was once in a while at first. Only recently have they become more frequent," Dominic explained.

"How frequent?"

"Three to four times a week? I wake up in cold sweats, and I am most times unable to return to sleep."

The doctor tapped a pen against his notepad as he said, "Do you take sleeping pills?"

"Nope, none of that. At first, I thought the dreams were as a result of the accident, trauma or something, but hey, I am no doctor."

"Is there something else you are not telling me?"

"No, I just feel like I am being watched every so often, especially when I am out."

"I see…" The doctor placed the pen down and leaned forward, "Mr. Gray, you know this was supposed to be your last biweekly checkup, if all your tests came out okay. And if all is well, your next checkup was to be in six months."

"But…?"

"All you have reported could be psychological, a result of the accident or other factors. Or it could be biological. First, the tests you did earlier all came out clean. You are great. So now, I am going to suggest that you have an MRI scan. If it turns up nothing, I will ask that you do as I say the first time you left the hospital, the recommendation that you trampled under your foot and refused to take."

"See a psychologist," Dominic frowned.

"Exactly. Within my jurisdiction, you are perfect, Mr. Gray, but you need to realize that good health goes beyond physical and biological wellbeing. Mental wellbeing is a key aspect of it. You just might be experiencing PTSD."

"Fine, fine, I hear you. How long will the MRI results take?"

"If we do the scan today, you can get the results in about a week."

"Perfect. So that means, I will become a former patient of yours next week, seeing how my next appointment will be in six months, you said?"

Dr. Perry chuckled. "You seem very excited to say goodbye."

"Oh, I am just curious if you will finally have the courage to ask Ana out then?"

"What?" the doctor's mouth fell open.

"I am pretty sure you heard me, doc. Come on, it is obvious you like Ana, a lot! And I am guessing that the fact that she is the relative of a patient held you back?"

The doctor averted his gaze to his notepad. Dominic chuckled and said, "Well, I am no longer your patient soon."

"Yes…" the doctor said slowly.

"Ana is beautiful and smart…" Dominic started but the doctor interrupted him.

"She is all of those things and more."

Dominic laughed, "True, true, I know I have an incredible sister. My point, doctor is this, if you keep dragging your feet, and refuse to take the chance, you might end up missing out on an incredible woman. Well, I will go get that MRI scan now."

"Do you think she likes me too?" Dr. Perry asked nervously.

Dominic chuckled as he patted the doctor's shoulder, "Did anyone else notice your haircut?"

"No?"

"Make of that what you will, good doctor." Dominic winked and headed out the door.

He grabbed his sister's arm before she could head back in.

"There is no need for you to see him. I gave him a little food for thought. Come on, I have a test to do."

"Food for thought? What are you talking about? And why do you have to do more tests? What did he say about the nightmares?"

"I will tell you all about it. One answer at a time, all right? Well, I will only answer questions about my health, nothing else."

Dominic filled his sister in on the conversation he had with the doctor about the nightmares and despite her protests, he refused to tell her what else he had been referring to.

"So, when do we get the results of the MRI? How soon can we know the situation up there in your head?" his sister frowned.

"In a week or so," Dominic told her with a smile. "You really have got to stop wearing that frown, Ana. I am pretty convinced that the scan will unearth nothing. As much as I do not want to admit it because of my dislike for psychoanalysis, I have a feeling that my problem is more psychological than anything else."

"You will see the therapist then, right?" His sister shook his shoulder, "Dominic Gray, why do you look so defiant?"

"I do not…" he rolled his eyes, "I do not look defiant. I am just deep in thought."

"You better not." She frowned at him. "You have to see the therapist, Dom. You cannot spend the rest of your life living with nightmares. That is no way to live. Do you understand me?"

"Yes, yes, I get what you mean, Ana. I get it, all right? Let's just take it one step at a time, all right?"

"Fine, you are right. One step at a time, that is the only option we have."

CHAPTER EIGHT

THE QUAINT TOWN *shone under the snowfall. The lights which were strewn over the houses called to those walking by. The town was truly a fascinating place to be as not only were the houses beautiful, but the hearts of those who lived within them were beautiful as well. It was a beautiful town through and through, on the inside and on the outside. And was it not the inside that was the most important of all? Indeed, Doverston was the best place to spend the Christmas holiday. It was a perfect home away from home for Yna and her siblings.*

A soft smile played on Dominic's lips as he flipped the last page of the manuscript his ghostwriter had sent to him. He looked up.

"Whoa…" he muttered. He was surrounded by a wall of darkness, which he could see through the glass walls of his house. She had sent the manuscript in the morning and he had become engrossed in it from the moment he started it. This was the eight story she was writing for him, but just like every other time before now, he was captivated by it again. But the most important of it all was how he had truly been transported to the town of Doverston where the story was based. He had felt like he belonged to the town and had not wanted to leave. It was one of those stories you wished would never end.

He sighed as he set the manuscript aside.

"Doverston, Massachusetts," Dominic said softly. He had never heard about it before. Sure, he was born and bred in New York city but he had travelled around the country, as well as the world a lot. It was probably a fictional town. Or was it?

He pulled his laptop close and typed it in. Dominic's eyes widened when pictures of the town popped into his screen.

"It does exist," he whispered. "And it looks very much as she described it, just what I pictured."

Dominic scrolled through the pictures of the city, finding that he was completely enthralled by everything he saw. It was quite idyllic indeed, and quaint. Dominic sighed and closed his laptop. He really needed to get some sleep. During his first appointment with the therapist earlier in the day, she had asked him to try to create a strict sleeping schedule and keep a dream journal where he wrote down every little detail of his dreams or nightmares that he recalled as soon as he was up. He rolled his eyes, just as he had rolled them the moment she said it at the clinic.

Anyway, the visit had not been as bad as he had anticipated. Maybe it was because he had already prepared himself for it in some way, mentally. It was either treatment for a brain disease or psychotherapy. He had known that the MRI results were the determining factor. And the results had come out clean as well, so it was off to psychotherapy for him.

Dominic ran his fingers through his hair. He had made his sister promise that she would only tell Eva but not their mom. If the woman heard about it, she was most likely going to be distraught and a thousand thoughts would run through her head. He could not put her through all that. He refused to. With the thought of Doverston on his mind, Dominic turned in for the night.

A little boy ran ahead of a woman on the street, laughing and waving at her. Whenever she was close to him, he ran ahead, laughing some more. The boy stopped in his tracks and gasped as he looked up at the Ferris Wheel.

"It is so big..." the boy whispered.

"I know, right?" the woman grinned as she pulled the boy into a hug. "Do you want to ride it?"

"I am scared," the boy whispered.

"You have no reason to be scared. I will be beside you and I will never let anything happen to you. I will never let anyone harm you. Never forget."

The woman stroked his hair.

"You promise?" the boy looked up at her with large eyes brimming with tears.

"I promise, little one. I have got you, always." She squeezed his hand tightly.

"Okay." The boy nodded. He took a deep breath and puffed out his chest. He smiled up at the woman and said, "I am ready. I have got this. I am ready to go on the ride now. Let's go."

The woman screamed in delight. She tugged his cheek gently as she softly said, "That is my brave, baby boy. So shall we go on our fun ride?"

"Yes!" the boy squealed as he pumped his fist.

Laughing the woman and boy headed towards the Ferris wheel.

They were enveloped with colorful bubbles and their faces were not visible. No matter how much he tried, Dominic was not able to see their faces. They were like a blur in a world separate from his and he was being kept away from them.

While he slept, a tear rolled down Dominic's cheek.

Dominic woke up the next morning and blinked at the sun-rays that were filtering into his room. He rubbed his eyes, surprised. Had he actually woken up in his own bed? When the day broke? He had grown so accustomed to waking up in the middle of the night, and he always ended up sleeping off in his study or living room.

He held his head in his hands. He had had a dream, yes, he knew he had. This time, it had not been a nightmare. He reached for the dream journal beside his bed and quickly scribbled all he remembered.

As he stared intently at his notes, Dominic frowned. Why was it all so familiar to him? A dream at a park. For the first time in so long, the nightmare had been dislodged from his mind and he had had a soft, but weird dream. Was it because of his meeting with the therapist? Nah, he shook his head. That was definitely not it.

He shut his eyes, the town had been so familiar. Doverston! It was the story. That was it. There had been an amusement park in the book and he had seen so many pictures of Doverston on the internet. But… it still did not make sense. What power did that town have that it was able to help him sleep well? Why was the town calling to him?

Dominic grabbed his phone and started searching for flights to Doverston, Massachusetts. He had to make his way there and see the town for himself.

Five hours later, Dominic was making his way through the arrival gate at the small airport that the town of Doverston boasted of. He pulled his phone out of his coat pocket and saw a voice note from both of his sisters, and several missed calls from them and his mother.

"Hey, where are you? Are you okay? You aren't answering your calls. Please call when you receive this."

The two of them pretty much said the same thing. He called Ana back first.

"Where on earth are you? You know, you are lucky that you are not a toddler, else all of New York police force would be out there looking for you," his sister scolded him.

"If I was a toddler, I would not be by myself, don't you think? That would be completely irresponsible of you, if you left a toddler alone."

His sister hissed, "Where are you? You didn't answer the question, Dom."

"Relax, all right? I came to Massachusetts."

"Massachusetts? Really? How come the sudden trip? There to see Wesley and Alex?"

"Uh… among other things, yes." He could not flat out lie to his sister but he also did not want to tell her the truth.

"Right… so you have a lot of things planned out then. Okay. Anyway, take care of yourself and stay safe, all right? And would you please call your mother and Eva? We have all been worried sick about you."

"Yes, I will. And I am sorry for the worry."

"Have fun and give our love to Wes and Alex, whenever you get to see them."

"Sure, I will." Dominic told her as his eyes darted around the airport.

Dominic found a quiet place and placed a call to his mother and Eva. Just like Ana, they had questions about his sudden trip. It was a good thing that Wesley was resident in Massachusetts. That was the major thing that succeeded in convincing them that everything was perfectly okay.

"Call us at intervals all right? Do not dare switch off your phone because you think we are bothering you. Do you understand, Dominic?" His mother asked him.

"I hear you, mom. I have no plans of ignoring you all. You make it sound like I always ignore you. I don't."

"Fine, fine. Just take care of yourself out there. I love you, son."

"I love you too, mom."

Dominic smiled as he hung up. He looked around the airport and checked the time. It was a little past 1:00 p.m. He had left New York around 7:00 a.m.. Well, now he really couldn't blame his family for worrying about him considering the fact that he had been off the radar for so long.

The man headed out of the airport and looked up at Doverston's warm sky. He had no idea how long he was going to be in the town but he intended to see if the Doverston in the book his ghostwriter had written was the same as the town he stood in at that moment. He was also very eager to find out why he was so intrigued by the town.

Dominic tilted his head as he realized something. That feeling of being watched was gone. Was it because he was in a new place or was it just something special about Doverston? Choosing to walk, he ignored the queue of cabs in front of the airport and turned into the main street. The only luggage he had with him was a small duffel bag and his backpack so he was perfectly okay with walking.

Dominic walked down the main street, fascinated by the buildings. They were just as idyllic and quaint as the ghostwriter had described. He chuckled quietly. When was he actually going to stop calling the ghostwriter that? Well, considering she was reluctant to tell him her name, maybe it was truly fitting to keep calling her that.

It was a warm day in Doverston and Dominic walked past a small group of children crowded around an ice cream stand, their cheeks flushed and their eyes twinkling with delight. Oh, the life of a child, so simple and so easy. Dominic let his legs lead the way as he began his one-man tour of the town.

Several hours later, Dominic's legs led him to a small café at the end of a street. He had been about to walk past it but the aroma from within pulled him back. As soon as he stepped in, the bells above twinkled and a waitress hurried to him.

"Hello! Welcome to Our café."

"Our café? That is the name of this place?" Dominic smiled.

"Uh huh, you know, the café belongs to all of us, the whole town." She winked as she led him to a seat.

"So, do we all share the profits of the café?" he grinned at her.

"Ah, you are not from around here, of course," she said with a knowing nod.

"I take it then that this is one of those towns where everybody knows everybody?"

The woman whose nametag said 'Lisa' shook her head, "Nah. Doverston is more like a town where some people know each other, and some people don't know each other. We are very close-knit but we also let people have their space. I think it is a perfect balance."

"Ah hah. Of course." Dominic nodded slowly.

"That joke has already been overused so a local would know," the woman smiled brightly.

"I see." Dominic nodded with a smile, "That definitely explains the blank expression I got in response."

She chuckled and said, "What do you want to have? Everything here is absolutely amazing so it would be quite hard, but if I were to recommend, I would.."

"Cocoa and hazelnut, please. And a lemon tart. Thank you," Dominic said as he handed her the menu.

"Definitely not a local," she murmured as she turned around.

"The locals are more polite, and wait for you to recommend all the best selections, I presume?" an amused Dominic asked.

"See? You are catching on." She hmphed and sashayed away.

Dominic chuckled and pulled off his coat. He had lost track of how long he had been walking but he had kept walking because he had wanted to see more and more of the city. He had gotten to see the local high school and elementary school, as well as the town hall. There was still a lot more he wanted to see, like the farmers' market, the local library, a famous book café he had seen online and the amusement park. The smile slipped off his face as he thought of the amusement park. Ever since he arrived in the town, it felt like he was being pulled into it like a magnet pulls on another.

Walking down the street had caused a warmth to settle in the pit of his belly, such that he did not think he had ever experienced before.

"Here you go. Your lemon tart and cocoa. Would that be all?" The waitress called Lisa set his order before him.

"Uh… how do I find the local library and a café called…" Dominic pulled out his phone and checked his notes, "BookADrink? Yes, that is it."

The woman tsked as she shook her head. She waved her hand and said, "This entire street is called Café street and across the road is Book street. Do you understand?"

"I feel like I should but I do not."

"Anything related to books is across the road on the next street. See? You are seated directly across from BookADrink and the local library is right next to it."

"Ah, I see.. thank you so much."

"Yeah, yeah," she winked and headed off to the customer who had just entered.

As soon as he had downed his tart and cocoa, Dominic paid for his meal and flew across the street. Wherever there were books, he always found his way there. Throw in coffee, and it was perfect. It was one of the reasons his mother's café was one of his favorite places in his city.

He stepped into a warm space with dark cherry and cream walls. The furniture looked like it was floating and was perfectly structured around a circle bookshelf at the center of the space. Bookshelves also lined the walls.

"Your first time here?" A voice asked him. Dominic pulled his eyes away from the bookshelves and found himself staring into a pair of familiar green eyes. How could he ever forget those eyes?

The woman smiled and tilted her head. It was not a smile that reached her eyes though. She said, "Can you hear me?"

Dominic blinked and mentally slapped himself into focus, "Uh… yes, it is my first time here. Hello."

"Hello. Welcome to BookADrink."

"Thank you. It is a really lovely place you have here," Dominic said softly. She is beautiful. That was what he had thought when he first bumped into her back in New York. And he still thought the same thing now. Wait, why did he keep seeing her wherever there were books?

"Thank you. You can give me your order while you take your time to look around. If you have any questions, please do not hesitate to ask me."

"You own this place?" Dominic blurted out.

"Yes, I do. For a few years now."

"It is unique."

She nodded slowly, "For Doverston, yes. Anyway, I love books and I love coffee, so I decided, let's do this."

"Yeah, but I think the concept is quite different from book cafes I have seen in other cities. You must have a very creative mind."

She chuckled and leaned closer, "Do you want to know a secret?"

"Uh…" Dominic smiled, unable to say a word..

"The café is shaped like a Ferris wheel."

"Oh…" Dominic's eyes widened.

"Uh huh." She grinned. "I used to go to the amusement park over at Fun street with my dad a lot when I was younger and…"

Her smile suddenly slipped. She cleared her throat and the light Dominic had seen was gone from her eyes. "If you are not ready to order now, you can just look around and let me know when you are."

"Okay, uh.. sure. Thank you."

She hurried over to a booth that Dominic had just realized was shaped like a Ferris wheel cage. He tilted his head as he watched her. She had looked so excited sharing about her childhood but there was clearly something there as a memory had immediately doused her light. He sighed as he turned to the bookshelf. Indeed, everyone was carrying a burden, some heavier than others, but a burden nonetheless. There were not many in the world who had it all, and lived like life was a vacation.

Books, books, everywhere, he thought to himself as he browsed.

The lights in his house went on automatically as Dominic made his way into his house. Tiredly, he settled into a couch and ran a hand through his hair. So much for spending the night and possibly the next few days in Doverston. He had been deprived of the opportunity because all the hotels and inns in the town were booked. The town was hosting a state sports game so there was no chance for people like him who just woke up one morning and decided to visit the town. He had been lucky to get a flight over there in the first place. Getting a flight that was heading back to New York late in the night, he had considered himself luckier in that regard.

His eyes darted around the house and he sighed. He was missing the warmth that enveloped him when he was in Doverston. He could not recall when last he ever felt that way anywhere in New York City. Well, asides when he was with his family, but in those situations, the warmth was from the people and not from the place. He had grown up in New York but he still felt like a stranger a lot of times, so why did a town he had never been in feel so warm and friendly. Maybe it was because it was a small town?

He pulled out his phone and sent a message to his ghostwriter.

I went to Doverston today. It is truly a lovely little town. It feels very familiar, like I have been there before.

A minute later, her response came in: *Doverston had that appeal. Everyone could relate to it. It was indeed a unique town, with an ambiance that could not be completely captured with words.*

'Was'? Her use of past tense caught Dominic's attention.

I guess it has been a long time since you went to Doverston?

Yes, a very, very long time. A lot must have changed – her reply.

I saw a lot of buildings that were quite similar to some you described. The town library still stands as well as the town hall, though they have undergone some renovations. Here are some pictures.

He attached some photos he had taken of the town as he sent the message.

Change, the only constant thing in life – the ghostwriter sent moments later.

Dominic sighed and dropped his phone beside him. He could not argue with that. He had experienced the effects of change so many times. Nothing in life was guaranteed as change was always constant indeed. He ran a hand through his hair. He really wanted to go back to Doverston. It had been tempting to head over to Wesley who lived two cities over but he had seen no point in showing up unannounced. He would return to Doverston when he could, definitely sometime in the near future.

For now, he needed to rest his legs and hit the sack.

CHAPTER NINE

DOMINIC FOUND HIMSELF back in Doverston two weeks later. This time, he ensured to book a room in an inn before heading down. He was not taking any chances. He did not know much about Doverston. Who knew if they had an entire calendar of events planned for the rest of the year? It was best to be prepared, he had learned the hard way.

Dominic welcomed the warmth that Doverston gave him once again. He walked around the town, enjoying the sights and the warm day. Dominic jumped out of the way as a child on a hoverboard flew by him, screaming, "Sorry, sir!"

With his jump, he ended up bumping into a petite woman in her fifties.

"I am so sorry," Dominic apologized as he helped her gather the documents that had scattered all over the sidewalk.

"Thank you," she said with an appreciative smile.

Dominic's hand froze over one of them as he realized it was a picture of an apartment. He looked up at the woman as he asked,

"Is this listing here in Doverston?"

She smiled wider and nodded, "Of course. Are you looking for a place in Doverston?"

'Well… I never actually thought of it but the idea is… feels… like a good one." Dominic managed to say softly. He had never thought of Doverston as somewhere he could make his home, but why not? It was a beautiful town and one he felt at peace in. He did not have that feeling of being watched whenever he was in Doverston. And very importantly, his nightmares had reduced ever since he found out about the town, even more so, since he visited. They were not gone completely but there was significant improvement. Now, his nights were filled with the boy and the woman at the amusement park. He still could not see their faces though. Whether the dream was caused by the book, or a figment of his imagination, Dominic did not know. But the one thing he could at least tell was the fact that Doverston was a place that he truly felt at peace in. The town was like his therapy.

"If you are not sure yet, how about you take a catalog? You can see if there is something you like, and we can talk later. Oh, and you see, my contact information is right there." The woman handed him one of them.

"Can I do that?"

"Of course," she grinned. "Doverston is a lovely place. I hope you do decide to come here, and even if you don't, I wish you the best wherever you head to."

She waved and hurried down the sidewalk. Dominic watched her for a second, before he looked down at the catalog in his hand. He felt good in Doverston, that was for sure. But he did not want to make a rash decision. He could not uproot his entire life just because of a warm and fuzzy feeling, right?

"So, what do you think? What did Alex say about it?"

"It is a good city, it is mostly peace-loving with no issues, except for some cases of petty theft and similar kind of trouble. Basically, Alex says there is no way on earth she can stay there because it is just too boring. It cannot be considered a crime-fest like where we live. That should tell you that the cops over there don't have much to do. In summary, it is a pretty safe town. It is very beautiful as well."

"Thanks so much man. I owe you one. You know what? I should take you and Alex to dinner, yeah, I owe you both dinner."

"Whatever. I do not believe that for a second. You have been in Massachusetts what? Three times in the past month and we have not seen you. I will not be falling for your lies, my dear friend."

"Oh, do not be too sure, my friend. I will surprise you."

"Ha!" Wesley scoffed. "I certainly cannot wait for the surprise. Now, are you very sure about your decision? It is a big one. I mean, you have your mom and sisters back in New York. They are not going to be too pleased with your decision, right?"

"Uh huh," Dominic said with a slow nod. "I am most bothered about my mom. I do not think that she will be thrilled about my decision to relocate."

"So, your mind is made up, huh?" Wesley asked.

"I think it is. You know, the more I think about it, the more I am sure and more confident about my decision."

"That is good then. You need to be very sure about your decision. And even if peradventure, you end up regretting this decision, it will be fine. You can just mark it down as one of the experiences of life and move on."

"And the chief advisor speaks again." Wesley laughed at his friend's words. "Anyway, I think this will be good for me. The few times I have been there, I can sense it and I know this is the best choice I can make for myself right now."

"Well, that is good. You just have to go ahead and convince your mom now. I wish you all the very best, my friend, because you have your work cut out for you. Convincing your mom is going to be a mammoth task."

"Don't I know?" Dominic sighed.

"Don't you know what?" A voice asked from behind him.

Dominic turned around to see Eva looking at him inquisitively. He scratched his head, "How long have you been standing there?"

"I just got here. Who are you on the phone with for so long? I mean, did you come to have dinner with your family or you came to make a call?" She quirked a brow.

"I am hanging up now," Dominic said, "I will call you later, Wes, and give you an update."

"All the best, man. Don't forget to let me know how it goes."

"Was that Wesley? Why didn't you bring the phone inside? I am sure mom would have liked to speak to him too. You did not have to have your call out here on the patio."

"Right…" was all Dominic could say. He wrapped an arm around his sister's shoulder. "Come on, let's go have dinner."

"Like you are not the one we have been waiting for. But, are you sure you are okay, brother? You look worried, like really worried."

"It is fine, I just have a few things on my mind," he forced a smile.

"Like what? You know you can always talk to us."

"Yes, and I will tell you all about it after dinner."

Eva looked at his face searchingly. She looked like she wanted to say something but seemed to think better of it, because she nodded and said, "Okay then. If you say so."

"Please don't mention anything about it to mom."

She shrugged, "What do I know that I want to tell her? Absolutely nothing."

"Would you prefer I faint from starvation before you decide to come eat?" Ana called to them.

"Oh little sister, even if you are starved of food, you can never be starved of love," Eva told her sister, winking.

"Oh really? You have to do this?" Ana tried to look stern but she could not hold back her smile.

"Oh yes, that is true. You and the good doctor had your third date yesterday, right? So…?" Dominic wagged a brow.

She shrugged and said, "If you must know…"

"Oh we must know," their mom said as she settled into her seat, causing them to laugh.

"Fine, fine, we have officially started a relationship, okay?"

"Well, that is not surprising," Dominic said, to which Eva and his mom nodded in agreement. "We all knew that was where it was headed. The two of you are always starry-eyed when you look at each other. Yours is like one of those love stories that just has to be."

"Exactly." Eva nodded, causing Ana to chuckle.

"There is something I have to say," Dominic told the women in his life when they were all settled in front of the television later that evening, cradling mugs of hot chocolate. They looked at him expectantly.

"I am moving to Massachusetts," he announced.

"Wow, that seems very sudden," Eva said quietly.

"It is not. I have thought long and hard about it. It is a quiet town and it is going to give me the peace and tranquility I have been craving for a while. While I have this amazing ghostwriter, I would also like to resume writing by the end of the year, and being over there, away from the hustle and bustle of the city is definitely what I need. I am actually considering a joint project with my ghost writer. I have all these plans, and the more I think about them, the more I realize that I do not want to do any of it here."

"Well, I think your peace of mind is very important, Dom. We will miss you a lot but I am very glad that you are finally prioritizing your health. It will be hard adjusting to you not being a stone throw away, but it is fine, I am sure we will all adjust to the five-hour plane ride. It is five hours, right? Wait, this place has electricity, right?" Ana said.

Dominic laughed, "Of course it does."

"Well, I agree with your sister. It will be hard adjusting but if this is what you feel is best for you, we will support you. You know we always will." His mother smiled.

"Thanks, everyone. I was really worried about telling you all, especially mom."

"I can see why," Eva chipped in. Her mother threw a glare at her, causing her siblings to laugh. "So what city are you headed to?"

"Doverston..."

His mother's smile fell and she gasped, "What? Doverston? Why?"

"It is a very safe city, mom. Alex says the crime rate is low and..."

"Anywhere but the west of Massachusetts," his mother said quietly.

"You cannot be serious, mom. I mean, a second ago, you were excited and..." Ana started.

"Anywhere but the west, all right?"

"Why?" Dominic asked quietly.

"I just don't like it there." She told them stubbornly.

"That is not an answer, mom. I understand you are worried but I will be fine. I love it in Doverston, it is warm and homely, and it is also closer to New York. My mind is made up, mom. So can you please be happy for me, and support me?"

She sighed and clamped her mouth shut. Dominic sighed and hugged her. Over her head, he exchanged concerned looks with his sisters.

CHAPTER TEN

A SMILE PLAYED ON Dominic's lips as he lifted his mug of coffee to his lips and took a whiff of the aroma. There was nothing like brewing your own coffee from fresh coffee beans you selected by yourself, the man thought to himself as he took a sip of the strong brew. His eyes were focused on the tree lined street which the large window in this living room looked out to. His smile deepened as five children in the neighborhood raced by on their skateboards.

"Hello, Mr. Dom!' The children waved at him as they sped by.

"Hello, kids! Have fun!" Dominic waved at them through the open window.

"You lots better be careful! Don't come back here with scraped knees and bruised elbows!" The neighborhood grandma, Mrs. Potts called to the children as she crossed the road, making a beeline for Dominic's house.

Mrs. Potts nodded at Dominic and pointed at his door as she got closer. Dominic grinned at the sight of the stern look on the woman's face as he headed to the door.

Dominic spread his arms wide as he opened the door. Cheerfully, he said "You look lovely this bright morning, Mrs. Potts. Is that a new scarf? It matches your eyes so well."

"Spare me the flattery, Dominic," she pouted as she marched into his foyer.

"Oh my, is something wrong, Miss Potts? Who on earth dared to offend you? Who dared to do that? I need their names and addresses," Dominic teased her.

"Oh you don't say," the woman frowned. She crossed her arms and peered closely at Dominic. "What happened last night, young man?"

"What could you possibly be talking about?" Dominic feigned ignorance as he headed into the living room. He plopped down on a sofa and pulled his laptop close to him, holding his coffee with the other.

"Do not try to pretend, Dom. She told me everything." Mrs. Potts was close behind him.

"I still do not understand what you mean. What could she have told you that made you this mad?" the corner of the man's lips tilted as he tried to hold back a smile.

The woman's blue eyes, which still shone so brightly despite her age, narrowed at Dominic as she said, "Did you or did you not tell that fine young lady that she is ill-tempered and a spoiled brat before walking out on her in the restaurant?"

"Well…" Dominic shrugged, "Not in those exact words, but I guess you can say it was something along those lines. And I did not exactly walk out on her. I paid the bill, and excused myself."

"So you admit it. Why would you do that, Dominic? Rita is a fine young woman with great character. I watched her grow up. She is very polite, sweet and kind…"

Dominic smiled ruefully and shook his head, "Oh, Mrs. Potts. All those words cannot be used to describe the woman I met yesterday. The kind and sweet child you are describing definitely did not retain her compassion, that is for sure."

"What?" The annoyed look on Mrs. Potts' face crumpled to one of concern and she settled into the seat next to Dominic, "What do you mean?"

"Uh huh. It is clear to me that she did not give you the full story. She clearly knew she was wrong, despite her insistence, and arrogance at the restaurant."

"What exactly happened between the two of you?"

Dominic sighed, "I only went for that date because of your insistence, Mrs. Potts, even though I did not want to. Still, I was going to be on my best behavior. Everything was going well. I mean, I already knew I was not going to see her again. besides the fact that there was no connection between us, the only topic your dear Rita could talk about was herself…"

Dominic trailed off and palmed his face. "Where are my manners? I am sorry, Miss Potts. Would you like some coffee? Tea? I had some really good flavored Ceylon tea. Would you like to try it?"

"Sure, sure," she nodded.

She let Dominic lead her to the kitchen. As Dominic set the kettle to boil, he continued recalling the events of the previous night.

"So there we were making small talk when the waiter arrived with the wine, then, the food. So the waiter fills our glasses, and she bumps into him, causing him to spill some wine on her hands. What does your dear Rita do? She jumps to her feet and slaps him right on his cheeks."

Mrs. Potts gasped, "No way!"

"Yes way, Mrs. Potts. You heard that, right. He was a poor kid, not up to twenty-five. And really, none of that mattered! Old or young, poor or rich, that is no way to treat another person. I tried to pull her off him, and she kept throwing insults at him, then she turned on me when I apologized to the waiter. She continued her rant and the manager had to see us. And of course, I told him the mistake was completely our fault. And that also did not sit right with her, so then, I told her she was ill-tempered and acting like a spoiled brat. I paid the bill for the uneaten food, and left after I was convinced that the manager would not let go of the waiter because of Rita's insistence."

"Oh my!" Mrs. Potts' hand flew to her chest. She gratefully accepted the cup of tea that Dominic handed to her, and took a slow sip. She sighed as she set it down. Softly, she said, "This is really good, but all you have told me has left me too sad to appreciate it. I am so sorry you had to go through that Dominic, and I am so sorry about her behavior."

Dominic sighed softly and squeezed the woman's hand affectionately. "It is not your fault that she is that way, Mrs. Potts. And it is fine, really. In life, we meet different characters. It was quite an experience."

Mrs. Potts shook her head and softly, she said, "How did such a sweet girl turn out to be so mean? She is always so polite whenever we see each other."

Dominic shrugged, "I really cannot answer that question. I really appreciate your concern and care, Mrs. Potts. I am truly grateful, but please, no more blind dates."

The woman frowned, "You say that as if you have been out and about on dates since you arrived in Doverston. This is your first date ever!"

"And I really don't want more," Dominic smiled sweetly. "I do not want to start what I cannot finish."

"I cannot sit back and watch you be alone," the woman said stubbornly, shaking her head, as if to buttress her point.

"Thank you, thank you so much, Mrs. Potts, but I will be fine," Dominic held her hand desperately as he pleaded.

"There are many nice ladies in town and I know a good number of them. I will get you hitched in no time. Don't you worry about it now," she flashed a bright smile as she patted his hand. It was clear that her anguish from earlier was gone and she was now rejuvenated.

"No, no, you are not listening to me. Thank you, but I do not want…"

"Oh, no need to thank me, dear boy. I am happy to do it. You are a good person and deserve to be with someone great too. I will find her." She finished her tea in a few more sips and stood up.

"No, you don't have to. Thanks but no thanks," Dominic said but he could see that his words were lost to her. Her eyes were twinkling like she had some bright idea up his sleeve. He had only known Mrs. Potts for two months, since the moment he moved into Doverston and she had come from across the street with a large platter of potato salad to welcome him to the neighborhood. But he had also been around her long enough to know she was a determined woman who always did what she wanted to do. At eighty-five, she was spry and involved in everything going on in the neighborhood, and knew a lot about the happenings in Doverston. There was a reason she was known as the neighborhood grandma.

"I will see you soon, Dominic dear. Have a great day, all right?" She waved and headed off cheerily, her mood a complete opposite of when she had arrived.

Dominic sighed. He was just about to close the door when he spotted someone at the end of the driveway waving at Mrs. Potts. It was Ian, the owner of the restaurant Dominic, who had had the catastrophic dinner the previous night. The two men had met each other at Ian's restaurant a week after Dominic's arrival in the city two months ago and they had hit it off right away.

An amused expression was on Ian's face as he got to the door, "Why does Mrs. Potts have such a happy expression on her face?"

Dominic shrugged, "Why do you think? She has found a mission."

Ian laughed as he shut the door behind him, "I told you that the moment you let Mrs. Potts lay her hands on your relationship life, it is over for you."

Dominic groaned, "What could I do? She asked if I have a girlfriend. Of course I could not lie."

"True that," Ian chuckled as he made his way to the kitchen. He called behind him, "And you are paying it for now. It is amazing, don't you think?"

"Whatever," Dominic grunted as he rinsed his mug and set it to dry. He tilted his head at the boxes in his friend's hand. "What is all that? What is in there?"

Ian grinned as he filled a mug with coffee. He nudged his head at the boxes and said, "Check it, go on."

"O…kay." Dominic gingerly opened a box and rolled his eyes when he was greeted with a void. "Really man? You could not simply say they are empty?"

"Where is the fun there?" Ian's grin widened. "They are for the food we are taking to the book club."

"What are you talking about?" Dominic scratched his head.

Ian quirked a brow, "Did you already forget, man? We are in charge of the food for the book club this week? And tonight is the meeting. We literally talked about going to the farmers' market this afternoon two days ago."

"Oh yeah, that conversation kinda rings a bell," Dominic nodded slowly, frowning like he was still trying to recall the conversation fully.

"Keep trying to think hard. Whether you remember or not, we are still handling it," an amused Ian told Dominic and bumped his shoulder.

"Well, I guess that did not work," Dominic chuckled. His eyes flitted over the boxes and he turned back to his friend, "Why exactly don't you have a bakery? That would have been so much easier."

"Very funny. You so eagerly volunteered you and I last weekend, now you don't want to bake. No one is getting out of this, my dear friend. Come on, let's take stock of what you have so we know what we need to get at the market."

Dominic settled into a stool and shrugged, "Come on, this should be fun. The book club is a lot of fun but you have to admit that the snacks that are brought can be not so great. I am trying to send a subtle message to everyone else to do better and put in a little bit of effort."

Ian threw his head back and laughed, while Dominic stared at him. When he had settled down, he looked at Dominic and said, "Oh man, what kind of book club were you in back in New York? The one where you have five course dinners at the end of it all?"

Dominic shrugged, "I never was a part of one. I never really was a people person."

Ian looked thoughtful as he said, "I find that hard to believe. You get on pretty well with everyone at the book club."

A soft smile played on Dominic's lips as he said, "I like the club and everyone there a lot too. They are good company. Perhaps, I have found my tribe?"

"Well then, tribesman, can we please get to work? I would appreciate it if we could draw up a shopping list anytime now. I do not look forward to the hungry stares of the tribe."

Dominic laughed as he raised his hand in surrender. "Yes, boss. Let's do this."

A few hours later, the friends were at the farmer's market. They split up, their respective assignments in mind. Once he was finished with his errands, Dominic waded through the sea of stalls, taking in the bustling sights of the market. The longer he stayed in Doverston, the more he loved the small city life. There was a part of him that wished he had moved sooner. Living here had settled in him a sense of peace and security that he had not felt for a long time, well, if he wanted to be more specific, since the accident. that feeling of being watched that had seemed to become a part of his everyday life was gone now. It had been just two months, but so far, he had no reason to regret the big and drastic move he had made.

Dominic stopped at a fruit stall, and frowned as he was not satisfied by what he saw. Something suddenly caught his attention from the other side. Grinning at the sight of the large apples spread out in crates in a stall across the path, he made to move around the stand when he bumped into someone.

"Oh, I am so sorry," Dominic apologized quickly. "Are you okay, ma'am?"

He stretched out a hand to help the older woman with her bag and handed it to her.

"Thank you.." the woman began to say as she accepted it from him. She was a small woman with thinning brown hair that was held back in a bun. Her brown eyes suddenly widened, and she gasped. The woman went as pale as a sheet, and Dominic placed a gentle hand on her shoulder.

"Are you okay, ma'am?"

She shuddered and backed away, and out of his reach. Still looking up at him, with an expression that Dominic interpreted to be a mixture of shock and fear, she nodded vigorously as she said, "Yes, yes, I am okay. Thank you."

"Are you sure about that, ma'am? You look really pale. Are you sure you do not need to see a doctor? Maybe have them run some tests? Your health should not…"

She interrupted Dominic, "I will be fine… thank you."

"But…." Dominic started saying but she was already hurrying off. His concerned eyes followed her as she hurried off. She stopped a couple of stalls ahead and spared a look at him. As soon as she saw he was still staring, she took off. Dominic did not stop looking until she was out of sight and he noticed that she had looked back a few more times.

"That was so weird," he muttered under his breath.

Deep in thought, he headed to the exit, the apples he had wanted to buy forgotten.

"Find everything on your end?" a voice asked beside Dominic who was still deep in thought.

It was a nudge to the side that jolted Dominic back to the present. He looked at his friend, confused.

"Where is your head at, Dom?" Ian asked Dominic.

"Nowhere. Here, of course," Dominic said quickly and headed across the street, Ian beside him.

"Did you get everything?" Ian repeated the question he asked earlier.

"Yeah, sure," Dominic nodded absentmindedly.

"Is something bothering you? Something happened?"

"I…" Dominic started, and his mouth clamped shut. He did not know how to explain it. "I just met someone who seemed very startled to see me."

"Huh? What are you talking about?" Ian raised a brow. "You know this person?"

Dominic shook his head and slipped into the driver's seat, "Maybe I am just overthinking and misinterpreting what happened. It's just, she turned white when she saw me, Ian, like completely white. I mean, at first, I thought she was sick, but… nah… that is not it."

"Maybe she is a fan of yours?" Ian suggested as he buckled his seatbelt.

"Yeah, I thought about it, but… nah… I do not think that is it. You didn't see the look in her eyes, man. That was not a look of excitement, or the look of recognition I get when someone recognizes me, or my name. It was something else. Sure, maybe recognition was thrown in somewhere in the mix, but I bet you, it was more than that."

"What was it then?" a curious Ian asked.

"Fear, I think. That woman was not just shocked, Ian, she looked terrified." Dominic shook his head. "But why? Maybe I am just overthinking it."

Ian tapped his chin thoughtfully as Dominic pulled away from the curb, "And you have never met this woman before?"

Dominic shrugged, "I doubt I have. I mean, while I love Doverston a lot, you know very well my social circle is quite small, consisting of just you, the book club members, and my neighbors like Mrs. Potts. I have been around Doverston enough to be identified in such a way. And that is the crux of the matter. That expression, it was tense, man."

"I think you should not think about it too much, man. Who knows? Maybe you just reminded her of someone she knew in the past. Remember my mom said you looked familiar when she first saw you, and she later said you have one of those faces that look familiar."

"I still find that ridiculous," Dominic shook his head stubbornly, remembering the encounter.

Ian smiled and said, "Look, don't think too much about it. Doverston isn't that big. If you ever meet her again, you can find out what the deal is. There is no use mulling over it, as there is literally nothing you can do."

Dominic nodded slowly, "Yeah, you are right. Yeah…"

CHAPTER ELEVEN

"THESE ECLAIRS ARE absolutely amazing, Dominic. I cannot believe that the two of you rustled these up." Mrs. Feathers, a chubby woman grinned as she piled her dish with several more. "You should definitely bring more of these to subsequent book club gatherings."

"Uh huh," Dominic managed to say as he took a sip of his juice.

"Who invited her?" A voice whispered beside Dominic. He chuckled as he looked down to see fourteen-year-old Alex frowning at the woman.

"Me, and I truly regret it now," Ian said with a slight shake of his head.

"You know, maybe I should start coming to this book club. I never knew there was quite a lot to be gained," the woman said as she smacked her lips.

"I think I'm going to be sick," Alex groaned and went in the opposite direction.

"You know, it is just as if you prepared all my favorite meals," Mrs. Feathers said as she reached for her fifth serving of chicken enchiladas.

"That is her fifth plate, Ian. Not everyone who is an actual member of the club has eaten yet she keeps piling her plate. It is not fair to everyone else, don't you think?" Dominic told his friend in a shout whisper.

"When I saw her out there and invited her to the lounge, I did not know she was coming in with two stomachs."

"Two stomachs? More like twelve stomachs," a voice said from behind them. The men turned around to see another member of the book club. It was Miss Ellen, a fiery elderly woman and retired reporter of the Doverston paper glaring at Mrs. Feathers. "I take it none of you boys are going to say anything because you are just too polite. Well, I will handle it then."

"I don't think you should…" Dominic started saying but the woman pushed through their midst and stormed over to Mrs. Feathers.

"You wolfing down all the food here is not a lovely sight, Gertrude."

"I beg your pardon? Are you calling me a wolf?" Mrs. Feathers gasped.

"Well, those were not my exact words, but if the shoe fits, I guess you have no choice but to wear it, right?" Ellen said with a shrug.

"Ellen! You are the rudest person I have ever met in my life!" Mrs. Feathers shouted and all eyes turned to the two women.

"And you are the hungriest person I have ever met!" Ellen snapped.

"Uh oh, this is not good," Dominic muttered.

"And this is the reason why not so great food is served at the book club, Dom. To prevent this kind of drama," Ian said pointedly.

Dominic shrugged, "I still have no regrets."

"Ladies, please calm down," Dominic and Ian hurried forward. "We can talk calmly. There is no need for name calling."

"Oh there is! I will not stand here and watch her insult me." Mrs. Feathers hissed.

"But you can stand there and fill your plate repeatedly, without any concern for others. I know you have always been selfish, Gertrude, but isn't this a little too much?" Ellen shouted right back at her.

"Oh grow up, Ellen! You have always been jealous of me because Carl chose me, not you! Move on! It has been over thirty years already!" Mrs. Feathers threw a jab.

Collective gasps spread across the room but Ellen was not one to be trumped over as she retorted, "Oh please, I never wanted Carl. He begged repeatedly that I forgive him but I dumped his ass right there for you to pick it up!"

"How dare you?!"

The flurry of activity that followed in the next few minutes had to be quenched by several members of the club.

It was a sighing Dominic that shook his head a few hours later as he dropped Ian off at home.

"It is funny how a plate of food led to so much drama," Dominic chuckled silently.

Ian laughed, "That is small city life for you, my friend. There is a lot of drama around the corner, even when you least expect it. Have a good night, my friend."

Dominic waved and pulled away. In a few minutes, he was at his house. That was another beauty of the small city life, the fact that he could get to his destination in a few minutes. The man let himself into his house, and locked the door behind him with three locks. As much as all he had experienced at Doverston so far was a strong sense of security, there was no way he was not going to keep his defenses up as he had always done back in New York. Like they said, old habits die hard.

After securing a glass of water from the kitchen, he headed to the second floor where he took his shower and settled into bed in his room. Dominic picked up the manuscript he had left on his bedside table and tapped it thoughtfully. Over the past few months, he had been in constant correspondence with the ghostwriter and she had always captivated him. She had a unique approach to storytelling, one that fascinated him. The last story he had received from her had convinced him of one thing he had been thinking about. He wanted to know more about her and start an actual work partnership with her, a partnership where she actually got credit for her work. He had been thinking of starting his own publishing company ever since he took this hiatus and he was strongly considering her joining him, if she would agree that was. She was a damn good writer, and if she chose to stay in the shadows, she certainly had her reasons.

Dominic picked up his phone and swiped to his messages. He stared at the last message he had sent to her the previous night when he finished reading the manuscript.

I would like to see you. Can we meet?

There was still no response from her. He sighed and set the phone down. He could not tell if she had not read it yet, or if she had just decided to ignore him. surely, they had a good enough relationship now, that she would not just ghost him like that right? He chuckled as he thought of the word 'ghost'. A ghost-writer ghosting. His chuckle deepened.

Dominic's phone buzzed just then and upon checking, a smile spread across his lips when he saw that it was the message he had been waiting for. She had sent her address to him and suggested a couple of dates. Dominic quirked a brow in surprise as he realized that she was living in the next town over. He scratched his head as he recalled the conversation they had while he was still in New York, when she said she had not visited Doverston in years. If they were just next to each other, why did she never bother to…? He shook his head. It was none of his business.

Smiling, he replied to her with a date that was convenient for him during the upcoming week.

See you then, Dominic. Came her reply.

A smile playing on his lips, Dominic settled in for the night. Less than an hour later, he woke up drenched in sweat. The man ran a hand over his face as he shuddered. Flashes and rainfall, that was all he remembered. And screams. He touched his cheeks and felt it was moist. He had been crying, but why. Dominic shut his eyes and sighed? Why? Why oh why? What on earth had triggered this nightmare? Ever since he first visited Doverston, the nightmares had reduced and had gradually been replaced by the clouded dream at the amusement park. While he could not understand the meaning or significance of the dream, he had certainly welcomed it more than the nightmares. It was warmer and more friendly. Gradually the nightmares had reduced, until they had ceased. He had not had a nightmare in almost a month. Why today then? What had happened?

The man sat up and took a sip of water. Now, there was no way he could sleep tonight. How did a good day end so badly? He pulled out the drawer of his bedside table and found the dream journal he had left in there weeks ago. There had been no point writing in it all this time as the dream had remained the same, no clarity, no difference. Well, now he had something new to write, he grunted.

Rainfall, screaming, pain, flashes. Dominic shut his eyes as he tried to remember more, to no avail. He tossed the journal aside and grabbed his laptop. He might as well binge watch a show if he was going to be awake all night, he thought, resigning himself to his fate.

"So, I found you the perfect woman. She is…" Mrs. Potts started saying the moment Dominic opened his door.

"Good morning to you too, Mrs. Potts," Dominic smiled at the woman.

She paused and quirked a brow, "Were you about to leave? Where are you headed off to?"

"I have a meeting out of town," Dominic told her as he grabbed his car keys.

"Really? Where is it at?"

Dominic smiled again and said, "Mrs. Potts… What did we say about boundaries?"

"What? What wrong did I do? Do you have a girlfriend you didn't tell me about?"

"No, I…"

"Have you set your eyes on a girl? Tell me, who is she? Do I know her? I can talk to her and…"

"Mrs. Potts, no, I have not set my eyes on any woman, and I do not have a girlfriend. I am headed to a business meeting, and will return later in the day. That is all. Can I leave now?"

"But…" The woman pouted. She crossed her arms and said, "Fine, go do what you want to do. You don't want to tell me anything? Fine, suit yourself."

"Thank you, Mrs. Potts! I will see you when I return."

Dominic said firmly. Still pouting, she turned and headed to the door. Dominic chuckled and headed after her. The woman was very dramatic, that was for sure. She was sweet, she was kind, but she was also very nosy. As much as he appreciated her kindness and care, he also liked his space.

Dominic headed to the car and was about to open the door when she called out to him again. He met her halfway.

"Are you feeling okay? Are you very busy these days?"

Dominic raised a brow, "What are you talking about?"

"Well… It is just that I have been noticing the light in your second-floor window, it is usually on late into the night. It has been like that for the past week or so. It was never like that."

"I see… do you never sleep, Mrs. Potts? Are you also the neighborhood watch?" A surprised Dominic asked. He did not know how to feel about the fact that his patterns were being studied.

"I can see you have a smart mouth today," Mrs. Potts frowned. "Well, if you must know, I have several late-night shows that keep me up late."

"You should not be sleeping late, you know that right?"

"You are one to talk." She scoffed. "So busy with work?"

"Have a good day, Mrs. Potts," Dominic called to the woman with a wave. Not waiting for her response, he slipped into his car and headed down the road.

Dominic found himself in the next town after a thirty-minute drive. *Welcome to Ravetown*, an old sign said as he drove in. The farther he drove into the town, the more Dominic felt how different it was from Doverston. The warmth he usually felt in Doverston was gone, and he suddenly had an eerie feeling running through him. The town felt familiar but he could not place why or what exactly it was that made him think so.

Dominic stopped at a traffic light and as he waited, his eyes flitted around. The buildings on both sides of the road looked very old, and it did not look like the town had seen much development. In a few minutes, he suddenly found himself driving into an area that looked completely cut off from the other parts he had seen. all around him were new and expensive buildings. It was such a big contrast.

Dominic continued driving, till he left the area behind and met a part of the town that looked more average. He checked the location again and sighed. The map had showed him some back roads that were about a ten-minute drive and placed him closer to his destination, but asides the fact that he had not wanted to try an unfamiliar route when going to an unfamiliar place, he had also wanted to see the town.

Soon, all the buildings gave way to a countryside lined by woods and farmlands. It was dotted with houses here and there. Soon, he could see no more houses in sight, only dense trees. Dominic swallowed hard. He had not seen anyone or house for over twenty minutes and he was already very bothered. All around him were towering trees. It had been over an hour since he left Doverston already.

Could it be a trap? He wondered as he turned into a cracked road. The trees here were so tall that they formed a canopy around, almost blocking out the sun. Was this a trap? Dominic wondered the farther he went. Was someone out to hurt him? He shook his head. As much as he was worried, he was also very curious about what was at the end of the road, or in this case, the forest tunnel he had found himself in.

Dominic finally emerged into an overgrown yard and found himself staring at a mansion that he was sure had once stood tall and magnificent. Vines climbed around the building, creating a home in the trellises. The man alighted the car and looked around. It felt very quiet, like there was no one around. Slowly, he headed to the door and gingerly, he lifted the knocker.

The door flung open in seconds.

CHAPTER TWELVE

A YOUNG WOMAN STEPPED out of the house, smiling brightly at him. She had long brown hair up in a ponytail and was wearing a brown maxi dress. She clapped her hands in delight and said, "Dominic! It is so good to finally meet you!

"Yeah! You too!" Dominic managed to say, trying to mask his shock. She looked way younger than he had expected, like she was in her mid-twenties. The moment she got closer to him, Dominic felt very lightheaded. He held on to the side of the house as he tried to compose himself.

"Are you okay?" she touched his arm. He shuddered. While her touch was icy cold, he felt warm on the inside. How was that even possible? He wondered.

She smiled softly, revealing a perfect set of pearly whites. "You have probably driven a long way. You must be tired. Come on in and settle down."

"Thank you." Dominic smiled appreciatively and let her lead the way into the house. The house felt cold and he had to hold his coat tighter around him. She smiled and motioned to a seat.

"I will get you some water."

Dominic settled down and his eyes darted around the space. It looked homey, yet at the same time, he had a sensation he could not place. It was an indescribable feeling.

"Here you go," the ghostwriter returned with his water which he accepted gratefully.

"Don't you feel a little cold here?" Dominic had to ask. She looked at him quizzically,

"Are you cold?"

"Uh… kinda, but if you don't have a problem with it, then it is fine."

"Oh nonsense. You are my guest, Dominic, so you have to be comfortable. I will turn on the heater and you should feel warmer in no time."

"Thank you," Dominic said in between sips.

When she returned, she settled across from Dominic and stared intently at him, that same smile on her face. Dominic shifted uncomfortably in his seat and said, "You know, I still do not know your name. I have always just called you my ghostwriter."

"My name?" she asked, tilting her head.

"Yes, your name. I told you mine but you never did tell me yours."

"Right, right," she nodded slowly. Softly, she said, "I cannot remember when last I was asked that question."

"Oh? You are always here?"

Her head jolted up and her eyes narrowed at him, "How do you know that?"

An eerie feeling ran through Dominic as he swallowed and said, "Oh, uh… it's just that I realized how close Doverston is to Ravetown, and I recalled you mentioned you have not been to Doverston for a while. So, I wondered if maybe you don't go out often."

"Right…" she said with a slow nod and her face softened. "I do not have reasons to go out. I only leave out of absolute urgency."

"You have quite the beautiful home here," Dominic's eyes darted around. "I guess you have everything you need here."

"It used to be more beautiful," she said quietly. She stroked the upholstery of the couch she was seated in as she said, "But time happened, and like with everything, time made it all fade away."

"Oh," was all Dominic could say. He tilted his head as he watched her. Her eyes were pregnant with a lot of unspoken words. She was wearing a smile but there seemed to be anguish behind it. He sighed. Indeed so many people in the world carried different burdens, some heavier than others. Maybe he could help her in some way? He wondered.

"Mirabel," She said softly.

"What?" Dominic raised his head.

"My name is Mirabel," she told Dominic.

"Oh, that is a beautiful name. I do not hear it often," Dominic smiled. "Can I call you Mira?"

A slow smile spread across her lips as she said, "It has been a long time someone called me that. Sure, that is fine by me."

Dominic nodded and was about to say something when his phone buzzed. He looked at it and saw that it was his sister calling.

"I am very sorry, I…"

"Oh it's okay," Mirabel smiled at him. She waved her hand, encouraging him to take the call.

He smiled in apology as he answered, "Hey, Ana, is everything okay?"

"Just calling my big brother to check on him," His sister's cheerful voice reached him. "Is it a bad time?"

"Kinda. I am actually at a meeting right now," Dominic explained to her.

"Oh? I thought your club meetings are not till weekends. When did it become a weekday affair? Today is Friday."

"It actually is not a book club meeting, Ana…" Dominic started slowly.

"What do you mean? Where are you then? Wait, have you started reaching out to publishers? I thought you said you wanted to take a break and…"

Dominic smiled apologetically at Mirabel and stood up. He headed closer to the kitchen and said, "No, it is none of that. I am meeting my ghost writer."

"Oh oh, wow. What? She flew into Doverston? That is some commitment, or wait, did you fly to where she is?"

"Uh… it turns out that we actually live quite close to each other, different cities, but still close."

Dominic looked up to see that Mirabel had picked up a book and was reading it. He squinted as he tried to make out the name on the book.

"Okay, that is cool then. You guys at some cafe?"

"Uh, not really. I am at her house."

"Are you insane?!" his sister's words thundered through his phone.

"Calm down, Ana."

"How do you expect me to calm down? You met up with a complete stranger! You have no clue who this person is, who she is really. All you both have done is exchanged messages! How can you be so reckless?!"

"Relax, sister. She seems like a really nice person, all right? I understand your concerns but there is nothing to worry about. She has been very nice since the moment I stepped in here."

"Sure… until she grabs a knife and sticks it in your back. You better not let her out of your sight for a second. For goodness sake, how can you be so trusting?! Sometimes I wonder who the older sibling is between us two. You know what you are going to do now? You are going to make it obvious so she knows that there are people who know your whereabouts, all right? So that she does not think you went there without telling anyone."

"Oh come on, Ana, I am not a child. I do not need to put up that act we used to do and…"

"If you choose to argue with me, I will let mom know that you went to the house of a complete stranger without telling anyone. You know she did not want you to go to Doverston in the first place," Ana threatened him. He could picture her stern gaze and set lips.

"You wouldn't…." Dominic tried weakly.

"You know not to dare me, brother, now say it to her just before you hang up. I want to hear it."

Dominic rolled his eyes and turned to Mirabel. He called out, "I am sorry. It is my sister. She likes checking in on me and wanted to know what I am up to."

"That is okay," Mirabel replied with a smile, "Take your time."

"Happy now?" Dominic groaned, as he returned his attention to his sister.

"Not a hundred percent though. I still do not understand why you didn't just decide to meet in a public place."

"She is not a fan of public places, or even people, and I kind of get it."

"I wonder why… oh I wonder why. What could she be running away from?"

"Okay, I am done with this conversation. Take care of yourself, and please do not tell Eva, because she is only going to end up calling me, and what she will be doing will be interrupting our conversation."

"Yeah, whatever," he heard his sister stubbornly say.

"You and I both know what that means, or rather does not mean, Ana. I need your word."

"Fine, fine, I will not tell Eva that you took yourself to the house of a complete stranger, who could be a potential serial killer. I will definitely tell our mother or sister any of that."

"And do not even tell your boyfriend," Dominic quickly added. He was not going to give his sister a loophole. She could be quite cunning and search for them, that was for sure, "In fact, tell no one."

"Yeah, whatever. Let me know when you get home. I love you. Stay safe."

"I love you too, Ana. Stay safe."

Dominic hung up and turned back to Mirabel, apologizing again, "I am very sorry about the interruption. Sometimes, my younger sister acts like my older sister."

"It must be nice," she smiled ruefully, "Having someone to care for you, and who you care for as well."

"Yeah… my family is very important to me," Dominic told her softly. He looked around the house, "How about you? Do you have any family around?"

She looked at him for a second and the anguish he had seen peeking through her smile was in full view. It was only for a split second, and it was gone. She said, "I did have people who cared about me, and people I cared for."

"Are they gone now? I am so sorry about that."

"I do not like talking about it, I hope you do not ask any more questions."

"Of course I won't. I am sorry if I made you uncomfortable. It was not my intention," Dominic apologized as he reclaimed his seat.

She nodded slowly and clasped her hands together, "You said you wanted to discuss some important matters with me. And you were willing to come all this way. I guess whatever you have to discuss with me is very important, seeing how you went out of your way to meet me."

Dominic smiled and he sat forward, "You are right. Indeed, what I have to discuss with you is important. You see, Mirabel, several months ago, I was working my butt off, never getting any rest, and surviving on caches of junk food."

"That is no way to live," Mirabel said with a slight shake of her head.

Dominic nodded in agreement. "I cannot say I didn't know that, but my work was so important to me and I could see nothing else but my work, and my family. Self-care and all that was really just a foreign concept to me."

"Something happened," Mirabel said, not as a question.

"Yes, indeed. I had a heart attack while I was driving, and my brakes failed. A coma for two months was the result of my overexertion."

Mirabel frowned, "A heart attack while driving might not be very uncommon, but your brakes failing too, that is weird."

"Yeah… that was my awakening, you know, literally. I got out of that realizing that I need to be more serious with my health and caring for myself. All-round health is what I am aiming for now. I was able to cut out some of the weeds in my life, so the accident was indeed a turning point for mee. Anyway, I decided to take a break, and this was when I contacted you. As the months have gone by, I have become more convinced of a decision. I want to start a publishing company and would like to sign you on, if you let me. I believe you are more than good enough to be in the light, Mirabel."

"It doesn't seem right, and it seems awfully familiar," Mirabel sat forward, her brows furrowed.

"Uh… what are you talking about, Mirabel? Did you hear everything I just said? What doesn't seem right? What is familiar?"

"You cut off weeds… What do you mean by that?" Mirabel asked, ignoring his question.

"Uh… just some people who never really cared about me, and who betrayed me, basically consisting of my friends who owned my former publishing company, and my ex-girlfriend. Why do you ask? Wait, did you hear me? I said…"

"And you cut them off after the accident, not before the accident," Mirabel said, more to herself than to Dominic.

"I feel like I am talking to myself here," Dominic said quietly.

"Did it not seem weird to you? Didn't you ever question it?" she asked again.

Dominic sighed and ran a hand through his hair. It felt as if she suddenly had lots of questions for him.

"Your accident, a heart attack and brakes failing. Didn't it bother you?"

He shrugged as he said, "Not really. It's not like I am in my twenties, that I would think it is so rare to have a heart attack. I am thirty-six, and I haven't given my body the best care. It was my body's way of reminding me that I am a human with blood flowing through my veins."

"And your brakes failed at that exact moment? Was it even investigated?"

"Well… at the time of the accident, I was unconscious as I already said. There was a record of me calling the emergency services because of the heart attack so I believe there was no investigation of the car. Wait, what are you getting at?"

She shrugged and sat back, "It's just weird that everything happened all at once. It is way too coincidental. It reminds me of something but I just cannot remember it right now, just like a lot of other things I cannot remember."

"My mother did question it a few times, but I do not think it is anything to worry about. Like you said, it was just a coincidence."

She nodded her head slowly, "I understand. It is not easy for many to accept the fact that someone might have tried to kill them. The thought that someone hates you so much that they would want you dead is not easy to fathom. It is okay to choose to live in denial. Sometimes, it is the best really."

"I do not think…" Dominic started but she waved his words away as she continued,

"Your proposal to have me become one of your authors, I am not so sure about it. I would love to do more projects with you, definitely, but I do not want to be in the spotlight. That, I am hundred percent sure about."

"Oh…" Dominic was caught off guard by how quickly she changed the subject of the conversation. He took a sip of his water and said, "Well, if you don't want to be in the public eye, how about we use a pseudonym? That way you get to keep your identity secret, but at the same time you actually get credit for your work? I think it is something you should think about, Mira."

"Okay, I have heard you, I will think about it. Now, can we talk about the projects? I actually have some ideas, and I recall you have some in mind for some projects too."

"Yes, yes, and I think this is the perfect start! We can write these sets together, and publish under your name and mine. Don't you think it is perfect?" Dominic grinned.

She smiled brightly. It was the first smile that reached her eyes. She tapped a thick folder beside her as she said, "We have a lot to talk about, so this is going to take a long while. Would you like to stay the night? And you can have breakfast before you leave? I am proud to say that I make the absolute best pancakes, the best you have ever tasted."

"Oh…" Dominic was taken aback by the suggestion, but he smiled widely. He was down for it. Besides the fact that he was looking forward to the amazing projects they could do together, she was great company. "Sure! Pancakes for breakfast, I like."

"Great," she smiled.

CHAPTER THIRTEEN

DOMINIC'S EYES FLEW open and he found himself staring up at the ceiling. He had been enveloped by a sudden chill, and he could not remember if he had been having the amusement park dream, or a nightmare. His head just felt cloudy, and it all felt fuzzy. He rubbed his eyes as he sat up in bed. He should probably try harder to sleep, he thought to himself. He was about to lay his head back on the pillow when he heard a rumbling sound, followed by a muffled scream.

Dominic jolted up and slipped into the soft slippers Mirabel had given to him earlier. He headed to the door and noticed a greenish glow through the crack under the door. What on earth was going on out there? Dominic wondered as he pulled the door open. Just as Dominic stepped out to the threshold, a scream pierced through the darkness,

"Don't come out! Don't come out!"

The greenish glow he had seen was suddenly gone and Dominic found himself surrounded by a dense fog. There was nothing in plain sight. He could hear loud humming and muffled cries but he could not see the source of any of it. He tried to move and back away, but he was frozen in the spot. He opened his mouth to speak but the action was futile as it was as if his lips had been sewn shut. What is happening to me? He screamed in his head.

Dominic's eyes widened and his heart jumped in his chest as a dark shadow floated toward him with great speed. The man tried to move his legs but they remained glued to the spot. Was this his end?! Suddenly, Dominic felt warmth on his shoulder and it was as if his body was defrosted. He turned his head to the side and saw the ghostwriter beside him. Her hand was on his shoulder, where the warmth had emanated from. Her brown hair was billowing as the fog intensified and a wind blew. She glowed green and she was the only source of light in the fog. Her brown eyes had become gray and it was as if she could see deep into his soul.

"Sleep…" she whispered in a bone chilling voice..

Dominic felt as if he was knocked by the wind as a powerful force flung him back into his room and he heard the sound of his door as it was locked. He was dropped on his bed softly, and immediately, he was out cold.

The rays of sun filtered through the gentle white curtains at the window, bathing the sleeping man. Dominic groaned as his eyes fluttered open. He rubbed the back of his head as he tried to make sense of where he was. Right! He nodded. He had spent the night at Mirabel's.

As he sat up, he winced slightly as he felt a throbbing pain in his lower back. He looked down at the bed. It had felt okay the previous night, or had he slept on the wrong side? The previous night… The images of a dark floating shadow and a glowing Mirabel flashed through his mind. Dominic shook his head, and he shuddered. What on earth was that? He held his head as he tried to remember whatever it was but all he could see was Mirabel glowing green and a dark shadow bopping in a dense fog. The man sighed resignedly. It had probably been yet another weird nightmare. So rather than the amusement park dream to get clearer, he was now having new nightmares. Just great.

He groaned and pulled himself out of the bed. It was not his house and he needed to leave. As soon as he headed into the bathroom, Dominic shuddered. He could feel the gloom he had felt last night in the house, even though he could not remember why he felt that way or what had happened.

"That must have been one hell of a crazy nightmare," The man thought to himself as he stepped into the shower stall.

He headed down for breakfast after freshening up and found Mirabel stacking a platter high with perfectly shaped pancakes. The sight of her reminded him of the glow he had seen, and he shook his head. *Stop thinking crazy thoughts, Dominic.*

"You are up," she said, the moment she saw him.

"Thank you so much for doing this," Dominic said as he hurried to help her set the table.

"Oh, it's okay. I don't do it often so it is nice to have the chance to do it. Thank you for staying back and trying my pancakes."

"The pleasure is all mine," Dominic smiled gratefully, and meant it.

"Go on, sit down. There is freshly squeezed juice and coffee. You can take your pick."

"Thank you so much," Dominic said as he filled a mug with coffee. He turned to her and said, "What about you?"

"Oh… uh… I won't be drinking anything. Water is just fine for me, thanks. Go on, try it and tell me what you think. Sit down, Dominic. Come on."

Dominic settled down and placed a couple pancakes on his plate. He placed it on hers too and set it before her.

"Let's eat together," he smiled and she nodded appreciatively.

"Oh my goodness! This is so good! How on earth did you get it to taste this way?!" Dominic exclaimed between bites.

Mirabel chuckled and watched him eat heartily, taking large bites. "I am glad you like it, Dominic. It truly gladdens my heart."

Dominic stopped mid-bite and quickly took a sip of his coffee, "Aren't you eating?"

"Oh, I am fine. I am full."

"You ate some while you were cooking?" Dominic inquired.

"Uh… not exactly. I am really full. Look, I made all these for you. Don't feel guilty and eat to your heart's content, all right?"

"Thanks, Mira, really. But I won't finish these. You can keep some in the fridge and later when you are hungry, you can warm them, all right?"

She nodded and smiled appreciatively, her eyes moist with unshed tears, "Okay."

"I am so sorry Mira, did I say something wrong? It was not my intention and…"

"No, no, you did nothing wrong. Your care and concern, it just reminds me of someone," she said with a rueful smile.

"I am truly sorry for opening your old wounds, sincerely I am."

She reached forward and patted his hand. Dominic noted that it was warm today unlike yesterday when he had first met her. The image of a warm hand touching his shoulder suddenly blinded him and he shut his eyes, trying to hold on to the memory but it was gone the next instant.

"Are you okay, Dominic?"

Dominic sighed and said, "I think I had a really weird dream, or nightmare, I really have no idea what to call it."

"Oh?" she looked at him thoughtfully, "What was it about?"

"You know, I actually do not remember, as usual. I just get fragments thrown into my head here and there, enough for me to know that it is none of the usuals."

"You still have the nightmare you mentioned to me some time ago? I thought you said they were gone."

"Until last week," Dominic shrugged resignedly, "They are not as frequent as before but they are back, definitely, so much so that my neighbor even noticed the change in my sleeping pattern."

"Your neighbor?" Mirabel raised a brow.

"Uh huh, a sweet old woman who does not know how to mind her business."

"I see…" Mirabel said with a small smile. "You seem to really be enjoying it in your new home."

"I am, truly. Most people there are very welcoming and kind, and they seem to have big hearts, like you."

A bitter smile played on Mirabel's lips as her eyes flashed with one of her many expressions that Dominic could not interpret. "All is not always as it seems, Dominic. Not everyone who puts on a smile or shares a drink with you, or gives you advice likes you. Be very careful. There is a lot hidden under the surface everywhere you go. If you do not want to get betrayed, tread carefully and do not trust all that your eyes see, and what your ears hear. Look out for what is not shown, and listen for what is not said."

"Thanks, Mira. That is definitely advice that I will take to heart. Wait, you sound so much like my youngest sister, Ana, right now. What on earth happened to you overnight?"

She smiled at him and said, "Be very careful, Dom. And be happy too. Live a happy life, all right?"

"You talk like we won't see each other again," Dominic frowned. "We are going to see each other soon, right? Right?"

She chuckled and motioned at his food, "You should be eating instead of talking so much."

"You have not answered my question," Dominic said softly as he turned back to the food. He felt a hand on his head and he looked up to see her patting his head. He chuckled and said, "How can you be so young and act so old?"

"You never stop with the questions, do you?" she raised a brow.

"You are one to talk. You had lots of questions yesterday, remember?"

She nodded slowly, "Indeed, that is true."

Dominic ate in silence for a few more minutes before she spoke again, "Dominic, remember to be careful. After your accident, you have to be very careful."

"I will be, I am. Please, don't worry about me, all right?"

"It is hard not to," She told him quietly, "You are quite stubborn, and obviously, very trusting."

"I will be fine. You too, take care of yourself. And I better see you the next time I come here, all right?" Dominic said sternly as he watched her. She smiled ruefully and looked toward the backdoor. Dominic's eyes followed hers to the door and he titled his head as he tried to figure out what it was she was seeing. Her eyes once again held that look of anguish.

He sighed and turned back to his food. He wished he could help her more. He nodded his head determinedly. He was going to make sure she knew that she was not alone. The only way he could do that was by checking on her regularly. She better be prepared for a regular onslaught of messages.

He was about to stab his pancake with a fork when he saw that the corners were curled inward, unlike the others. Dominic chuckled and said, "Ooh… ear cake."

"What?" he heard a soft gasp from Mirabel. He looked up to see her staring intently at him. "What did you say?"

"Ear cake," he pointed at the pancake.

"Oh… uh.. why did you call it that?" It was the first time he was finding her at a loss for words since he met her.

Dominic shrugged, "I don't know. I have always called pancakes that end up this way ear cakes for as long as I can remember. See? The edges are like ears."

"Yes, yes," she nodded slowly.

She remained quiet for the rest of Dominic's breakfast.

The words Mirabel said when Dominic was about to leave surprised him.

"Can I hug you?" she had asked softly.

Dominic smiled and nodded, "Of course."

She pulled him into a warm embrace that left Dominic feeling secure and enveloped, like he was wrapped in a blanket.

"Take care of yourself, Mira. I will be seeing you soon."

"Take care of yourself, Dominic," she told him with a wave.

In his rearview mirror, Dominic saw Mirabel standing at the front of her house. The farther he went, the smaller she became, till he could no longer see her. The man felt a sinking feeling in the pit of his belly. He suddenly missed her and could not help feeling like a part of him was gone.

CHAPTER FOURTEEN

DOMINIC PULLED INTO his driveway and turned off the ignition. He stifled a yawn as he alighted his car. He oddly felt like he had not slept all night and his back kind of hurt. He shook his head as thoughts of the weird-ass dream he had the previous night occurred to him again. He could not help but wonder if they would ever stop, his crazy dreams and nightmares.

Once he let himself into his home, he took off his shoes, shrugged off his coat and headed to the kitchen for a much-needed glass of water. He had not planned to spend the night over at the ghost writer's but he was certainly glad he had made the decision. She was a sweet soul and seemed like someone who had a good heart. He was truly glad to get the chance to know her.

Dominic quirked a brow when he noticed the green beeping light of his answering machine. Who on earth would send him a message on his answering machine when it was so much quicker to call his phone? Weird. He pressed the button to listen and a very familiar voice filled the room, a voice that sounded very displeased.

"I can see that you have decided to start avoiding me, because there is absolutely no reason why you would ignore my calls for several hours, but that is fine, just perfect. It is a perfect way to treat your mother, that is for sure."

"Oh my goodness," Dominic muttered. "When did she call me?"

He pulled his phone out of his pocket and his mouth formed an 'O'. it was switched off, but that was weird. When exactly had that happened? He had used it just the previous night before sleeping. He had not bothered to check that morning, but he had had enough power before sleeping. He pressed the power button and his phone powered on. Dominic was greeted with a battery percentage of 80%. So weird, he thought to himself as he swiped to call his mother.

He realized the voice message had finished and replayed it to hear what else she had said.

"Oh, and by the way, just like I said before, I will continue to repeat it. I do not see why you had to uproot your life and move over there. Can you please come home now? I just have a bad feeling, all right? I don't anything good will come out of this. It won't end well, son. Please come home. Or move to somewhere else. Why does it have to be there? My instincts tell me this was a bad choice, all right?"

Dominic sighed and his hand froze. Deciding against calling, he quickly typed a message and sent it instead.

I am fine mom. I am sorry I missed your calls. I am not avoiding you, I am just quite busy. I will call you soon. I love you, mom.

He tossed his phone on the sofa and headed back to the kitchen. The sound of his doorbell made him sigh in exhaustion. He just did not have the strength for social interaction. Dominic felt drained.

Seeing who was on the other side of the door made Dominic sigh deeply. Why on earth did it have to be now? The man backed away from the door as he contemplated ignoring the guest. Before he could make a decision, a voice accompanied the doorbell.

"Dominic, I know you are in there. I saw you drive in a few minutes ago. Surely, you cannot be sleeping now."

"Definitely no boundaries," Dominic muttered under his breath as he opened the door. Rather than step aside to let her in as he always did, he blocked the entrance with his body as he said, "Good morning, Mrs. Potts. What can I do for you today?"

She frowned slightly and tilted her head toward the entrance, "Are you not going to let me in?"

"I am actually about to head out, so no, I can't," Dominic said in the sweetest tone he could muster without gagging.

"Hmm.. I see. You were not home last night, and that was contrary to what you said."

Dominic nodded slowly, "I know what I said, Mrs. Potts, and I decided not to come back to my own house. Is that suddenly a problem? After all, it is my own house and my decision to do as I please, right?"

"Indeed it is," she said with a slow nod. "Anyway, where did you sleep then?"

"I have to go now, Mrs. Potts, as I already told you. I have quite a few appointments today so the earlier I get my day started, the more productive I will be. On that note, I will see you sometime. That okay?"

"Well, I wanted to…" she started saying but Dominic cut in as he said,

"Well, since we are in agreement, I will see you around then. Bye, Mrs. Potts."

Not waiting for her response, he slipped back into his house and locked the door. Dominic stood at the side of the door, looking out through the peephole, and he could see her still standing there, her lips twitching. He had no idea what she was thinking but he did not need a soothsayer to know that she was certainly not pleased with what had just happened. Well, that was too bad. He needed her to stop monitoring his life and hovering over him. While he appreciated her kindness, and knew they were from a place of care, it was already becoming overbearing and he sincerely needed his space. After listening to that voice note form his mother, entertaining Mrs. Potts was the last thing he could do. He needed to run as far away as he could from her right now. He looked back to the peephole and saw she was gone. He breathed a sigh of relief.

Now, he could finally breathe and do what he wanted to do. He headed up the stairs to his room and just as he was about to pull apart his curtains, he saw a flash in the window across the street. Dominic narrowed his eyes. The person was trying to stay hidden behind the curtains but he could see it. He had not succeeded in getting rid of Mrs. Potts as he had victoriously thought a little while ago. He had to get out of there, he thought through gritted teeth. Shaking his head, he headed in to get a shower, and figure out what he needed to do next.

"Well, you do have yourself to blame," Ian chuckled.

"Really?" Dominic rolled his eyes and took a sip of his iced tea.

"Well, it's true. You were the one that let the old woman onto your space I'm the first place. If you had not, surely she would not feel the need to control your life and poke her nose in your affairs. You gave her the gate key."

"Simple acts of kindness, and being polite, that was all I did. I certainly did not anticipate this would be the result," Dominic rolled his eyes. He tapped the edge of his table as he said, "She is literally in all my affairs, even watching me from across the street. Come on, who does that?"

"A bored person who considers herself the matriarch of the street," Ian said and threw his head back in laughter.

"Very funny," a sarcastic Dominic punched his friend's shoulder lightly. "What a way to support me."

"Oh, I am supporting you, this is moral support. Look man, you have already ensnared yourself in the net and it certainly will not be easy for you to run away. But it is not impossible, don't worry."

Dominic rolled his eyes and picked up his phone, "I can see that I am just wasting my time having this conversation with you. All you do is laugh, rather than give me solid advice. What a good friend you are."

"You know what the best thing you could do is?" Ian suddenly asked. His smile was replaced by a serious look and he stared at Dominic intently.

Dominic quirked a brow as he stared back at him, "What is it? What do you have in mind?"

"You could move out of that neighborhood," Ian announced and he burst into laughter again, tapping his legs hysterically.

"I can see I am talking to a mad man. I cannot believe I fell for that. I actually thought you were about to say something sensible."

Ian dabbed at his eyes, wiping away tears of laughter. He finally said, "Look, the only thing you can really do is to be firm with her, right? Let her see that you do not want her in your business. While you appreciate her care for you, it has now become overbearing. You need to directly shut down her actions without hesitation. Right now, you keep humoring her, and if anything, it gives her the motivation to continue. You keep fueling her up, my friend."

Dominic shook his head and he ram a hand through his hair, "She is a really sweet old lady, and I really don't want to be impolite to her. I am trying not to be but…"

"You have clearly been doing a good job of it, seeing how she has been more than empowered to dig into your business. Soon, she will acquire a key to your home. I am surprised she doesn't have one yet." An amused Ian said.

Dominic sighed, "Let's stop talking about it. I only feel more annoyed the more we hammer on the issue."

"Okay, let's change the topic. But first, where exactly did you go to?"

"I don't understand," Dominic stared at his friend.

"Yesterday, I mean. Where did you sleep? Wait a minute, do you have a girlfriend? Who is this girl and why don't I know who she is?"

"Don't be ridiculous."

"But…" Ian started when the jingling sound of someone entering the restaurant resonated through the space.

The two men looked up and Ian jumped to his feet to the woman who had just walked in while Dominic looked on curiously.

"Eleanor! When did you get back? You look more radiant than ever!"

The woman smiled brightly, revealing a perfect set of whites. "Ian, you flatter me all the time. You do realize that I am five years shy of sixty, right?"

"And you do not look a day older than thirty," Ian was quick to reply.

The woman laughed, "You should get yourself a girlfriend and shower her all these compliments, not me."

"Oh Eleanor, are you now part of the brood of women in Doverston who want to see me married off?"

She chuckled, "To see you happy, yes."

The woman tilted her in the direction where Dominic sat, watching them quietly.

"Who is your friend? I haven't seen him around town." Before Ian could respond, the woman waved at Dominic, smiling as she said, "Hello."

Dominic stood up and got closer to them, "Hi."

"You must be new in town. I'm Eleanor." She stuck out a hand and Dominic shook it.

"Yeah, Dominic moved to Doverston, about two, three months ago?" Ian explained.

"Well, nice to meet you, Dominic. How do you like our town?"

Dominic nodded slowly as he said, "Doverston is very peaceful and calm."

She smiled and nodded, "It is one of the things we take pride in, and we always want it. Peace and calm, we strive to ensure Doverston is peaceful."

"Sure."

"It is very nice to meet you," The woman nodded to Dominic. She turned to Ian and said, "So, Ian, I will be needing 100 lunchboxes."

Dominic quirked a brow while his friend grinned as he asked, "Where's the party?"

"The elementary school baseball finals is this weekend, you know."

"Ah, understood." Ian nodded and gave her a thumbs up sign. "I will have them delivered to the school then."

"Thank you," she flashed a smile as she handed her card to Ian.

When she had left, Dominic turned to his friend as he asked, "How many children does she have in elementary school that she needs 100 lunchboxes?"

"What?" Ian grinned and shook his head, "Eleanor is buying them for all the children. She usually does such things, you know. She loves kids a lot."

"I see…" Dominic nodded slowly, "So who exactly is she then?"

"You really don't know anything about this town, do you?" Ian shook his head at his friend. "Anyway, Eleanor is very important, all right? She has helped a lot of people and made such an impact in this town. She cares a lot."

"So, like a younger version of Mrs. Potts," Dominic said with a slow nod.

"No, man, she is a philanthropist," Ian corrected him with a groan.

"Right, right," A now disinterested Dominic said as he turned his attention to his phone/

"I am telling, you my friend. She is a good person with a good heart. You would never even know how wealthy she is because she does not look down on others. You know that housing estate in the southern zone, her company built it and offered the apartments at subsidized rent to homeless and indigent people."

Dominic nodded slowly, "Nice of her. Anyway, I got to go now. I need to stop by the repair shop before it closes."

"What are you going to do at the repair shop? Something wrong with your car?"

"No, nothing of that sort. I just have something to do there. See you later, man."

He was headed to the door when his friend called him back. Dominic stopped and turned around.

"I just remembered, there is an event at the library next week. Clear you schedule. I think it is something you would like as you will get to know some more about Doverston and its history."

Dominic contemplated it for a moment, and he nodded, "It should better be worth it then. See ya."

About ten minutes later, Dominic was pulling up to the curb in front of the car repair shop. From where he was parked, he could see the kid. He was an eighteen-year-old boy that he had met at the repair shop when he first arrived in Doverston his car in for servicing. It had been his first time at the shop and he had met the boy. He had later met him at the book club, where the boy was still a member. The boy was bright and chatty, so they had easily struck a conversation in their second meeting, during which he found out that the boy was aspiring to be an author. Unfortunately, he had also fallen into the hands of some crooks who posed as publishers and swindled him, of money and his work, publishing the latter as their property. While many would not fall for the scams the kid had fallen for, Dominic could see how the boy had been fooled. He was naïve and had no idea how the world was, especially the cutthroat literary world. If you were not in it, you really would not know.

The kid was working at the repair shop so he could save up for college. With reluctance, he had finally agreed to send one of his manuscripts to Dominic. Despite the fact that he was a renowned author, he had still been very reluctant to take the chance on Dominic. It was even that knowledge of Dominic's identity that had fueled the boy's hesitance. Dominic had seen the doubt and fear in the boy's ears. He had been able to hear the thoughts going through his head, 'What if he steals my work? There is nothing I can do as no one will believe me. He is famous and honored and I am just a mere boy working at a repair shop'. The boy had finally decided to take the leap and sent it to him. That was a week ago.

Dominic alighted his car and lowered his head as he headed into the building. The sun was scorching. The weather was so weird these days.

"Welcome to B repairs," The boy said as he turned around. His eyes widened when he saw Dominic. He gasped, "Mr. Gray! What are you doing here? Is there a problem with your car already? That is not good."

"I am actually here to talk to you about your manuscript."

The boy gasped, and his eyes widened.

"You are surprised, you actually look surprised. You thought I was going to run off and claim your work as mine, right?"

The boy's eyes lowered and softly, he said, "I am sorry, Mr. Gray."

"Please, don't be. You have already been bitten so many times. I do not blame you for having guard up. It is what I would do if I were in your shoes too. There are bad guys out there, Eric, just as there are good guys. It is good to always be alert, but also be careful so as to mistake the good for bad, and vice versa."

The boy nodded and smiled softly, "Thank you very much, Mr. Gray."

"And you are still calling me Mr. Gray. I asked that you call me Dominic," Dominic smiled softly as his eyes flitted around the space.

"I just cannot get used to that, you are my role model, Mr. Gray, it is impossible."

Dominic smiled and he checked the time, "It is your lunch break now, right? Can we sit for a little bit. I have something to discuss with you."

"Okay, sure." The boy went around the counter and sank into one of the chairs in the waiting room.

"So, I read through your manuscript." Dominic looked at the kid and he could tell that he was holding his breath. His eyes were large and hopeful and Dominic felt glad that he was going to be delivering good news to him. "You have potential, Eric, lots of it. Your work is good, exceptionally good, and if you let me, I will like to sign you up to my publishing company. We have not kicked off yet but shortly, we will. Now, you can take your time to think about this decision. Then, you can let me know and a contract will be drawn and…"

"I agree. Of course, I agree," The boy said excitedly. "Thank you so much, Mr. Gray!"

"I know you are excited but I want you to take your time to think about it, Eric, all right? And when the contract is drawn upon your agreement, if you still want to, you should also read that thoroughly. Okay? Take the time, think well, with a clear head."

"Okay, but I am more than sure, Mr. Gray, but I will. Because you have said so, I will think some about it. My father is going to be so pleased! He has been one of my biggest supporters. Thank you so much, Mr. Gray. Thank you for being the good person that I have always thought you to be, thank you for preserving the image of you I have always have. And thank you so much for this opportunity." Eric grabbed his hand as he thanked him profusely.

"That is okay, Eric. Here is my card. Think about it and discuss it with your family, all right? The slot is not going to run away. And know that whatever decision you make should be for yourself, not me. I will respect it and support you in any other way I can. Is that okay?"

"Thank you so much, Mr. Gray."

Dominic smiled and stood up, "I will take my leave now. I have some appointments to handle."

"Thank you, Mr. Gray," The excited boy called out to Dominic as the door shut behind him.

CHAPTER FIFTEEN

"**H**EY, WHERE ARE you at, man? The event has already started." Ian nagged.

"I am coming, I'm coming. Hold your horses, all right?"

"Well, you better be fast. I would really like us to not be late," Ian added.

Dominic sighed as he got out of his car. He looked up at the familiar building that housed the town library. "What is this event even about? You didn't give me any details."

"It is actually a Timeline Event, it shows the history of our town and those that helped build it," Ian explained.

"O...kay, and I need to be here because?"

"Stop being rude and come in," Ian hung up.

Dominic rolled his eyes and headed into the building, shaking his head. He raised his brows, impressed at what had been done to the library. The entire ambiance was different and a lot had been readjusted to fit the event. On the walls were hung several pictures. The farther you moved in, the quality of the picture became better, changing from black and white to colored. There were stations next to each figure, which gave more information about who they were and their contribution. Dominic felt as if he was at an art gallery.

"Ah there you are. Finally!" Ian grabbed Dominic's hand. "Come on, I want to introduce you to someone."

"I have a feeling I will not give a hoot about this someone," Dominic pulled his arm out of his friend's grasp.

"Oh stop being incessantly stubborn, man. You will thank me for this."

Before he could protest any further, Dominic found himself standing in front of two, blonde women,

"Dina, meet Dominic, my very good friend. Dominic meet Dina. We went to high school together. Dina is a vet and she just recently moved back to Doverston. And Alice, I bet you remember Dominic, right?" Ian introduced Dominic to the taller one. Dominic realized then that he had met the other woman once at Ian's restaurant.

"Because there are so many sick animals who need her attention here?" Dominic finished his friend's statement with a question that earned him a glare from his friend. The two women laughed and Dina said,

"You really are funny, Dominic, just like Ian said."

"Oh really? Ian has been talking about me, I did not know that," Dominic said, staring pointedly at his friend who averted his gaze.

"Oh he has, only good things though," Dina winked at him.

"I am sure, seeing how you were interested in meeting me," Dominic started. Before he could continue, Ian threw an arm around his shoulder, saying, "Come on, Dominic, why don't we get some drinks for the ladies? Let us be gentlemen."

Quietly, Dominic let Ian lead him away. Once they were out of earshot, he turned to his friend, "So, now I have to be wary of both you and Mrs. Potts? This life sure is interesting."

"Oh stop exaggerating, man. Dina is a very lovely person and I have a feeling you both will hit it off."

"I should have known something fishy was going on when you insisted so much that I come today. I certainly did not know about this new matchmaking career that you have picked up. Am I your first client?"

"Oh stop being saucy. Look, after Alice met you, she was very excited and mentioned you to Dina, going on about how you both would be perfect for each other. I do see what she sees and since she was interested, I decided to hook you both up. You should thank me."

"All I am hearing now is that I was the only one unaware of this ridiculous little scheme. Well, thanks for the offer, but no thanks. Dina seems like a wonderful enough lady, but I am not interested. Do tell her that for me, seeing how you have handled everything else perfectly up till now. On that note, I am going to take a quick look around and get out of here. Ciao."

Ignoring what his friend was about to say, Dominic turned around and headed into the crowd. He stopped in front of a colored image of a man that looked wealthy but cheerful. He looked back at the images he had just went by, all rich but looking cold. This was the first different one he was seeing. He titled his head as he stared closely. Why did a man from 1990s' Doverston look so familiar to him?

His eyes went down to the name, reading it aloud to himself, "Gerald Woods." The plaque under his picture said that he had died in 1999.

Woods, he tapped his chin. Dominic leaned forward as he read some more. Together with his best friend Leon Cooper, Gerald had founded the first paper company in Doverston in 1970, when they were just twenty-five-year-old boys. They had gone on to create multiple businesses, such as the first department stores in Doverston and a chain of bakeries.

"Wow," Dominic whispered.

"He was loved by everyone. They both were." A voice said from behind Dominic. He turned around to see Ellen.

"Ms. Ellen, right… you worked at the paper, right? So, you must have known them closely."

"Indeed I did. Those two were good men with a sense of integrity. They loved their families and the people of this town." She looked up at him and smiled, "You know, the first time I saw you, I remember how shocked I was."

"Shocked?" He quirked a brow.

She nodded slowly, "You remind me a lot of a younger Leon, handsome and kind. You look so much like him, you know."

"Leon…?" He followed Ellen's finger as she pointed to the picture next to Gerald's. He had not noticed it at first. Dominic stopped in front of it and found himself staring at a man who had a million watts smile. He saw a flash and winced as he held his head. His head had suddenly started to throb. He raised his eyes and met the man's eyes. They were kind eyes, eyes that he felt he had seen a long time ago, but also very recently, but he was failing to pull up the memory. He tilted his head as he saw what the plaque said. He had died in 1998, one year before Gerald Woods."

"He is dead too," Dominic said, more to himself than to anyone.

"Yes, these two friends died a year apart from each other, a great loss to Doverston. It was as if they were always connected, you know. Their wives both died in 1991, in a plane crash, and then, that happened to them. After so much tragedy, we faced more as we had to still deal with…" Ellen suddenly trailed off. She shut her eyes tight, like she was trying to drive away a bad memory.

"Deal with what?" Dominic asked but Ellen smiled softly at him and said,

"It is sad to see how many have forgotten these good men that were part of the foundation of our great town. Enjoy the rest of your night, Dominic."

She headed off before he could reply. Dominic sighed and turned back to the picture of the two men who had contributed significantly to the growth of Doverston.

"Who owns the paper and all the businesses they left behind then?" He muttered under his breath. "Their family?"

He was quite curious to know what had become of everything the men had built. Knowing he would not get any answers from staring at the photos. Dominic backed away and moved into the next section.

"Mr. Gray!" A voice called to him.

His eyes darted around as he tried to find the source of the voice. He set his eyes on Eric who was walking to him, an elderly man behind him. The man was a few inches taller than Eric, and he looked exhausted. Dominic sighed. There were so many people out there having a hard time with life. So many times, he wished he could help every one of them.

"Mr. Gray, this is my father, Sam Dale" Eric smiled as he introduced the men to each other.

"Thank you so much for what you are doing for my son. Kind people like you are truly rare," The man stretched out his hand, and the two men shook hands. Dominic could not help noting that despite his frail appearance, his grip was still quite firm.

"It is my pleasure. Besides, this is an opportunity he got due to his hard work, diligence and creativity. He was the one that put in the work."

"Still, you were the one that saw the potential in him. I don't know if Eric has told you but he has run into a lot of problems while trying to tow this path. I have always encouraged him, telling him not to give up. And I am truly glad that all his efforts have been paid off. Thank you Mr. Gray."

"It is truly my pleasure, Mr. Dale. I presume then that Eric will be joining my company?"

"Yes, yes, without a doubt," father and son said in unison.

"Well, I am very thrilled to hear that. I look forward to our partnership," Dominic told them with a smile.

Sam Dale placed a hand on Dominic's shoulder and said softly, "Please take care of my son, Mr. Dominic."

Dominic opened his mouth to speak but he was suddenly flooded with an unclear and fuzzy memory, a memory made up of shadows. The taller shadow placed an arm on the shoulder of the smaller shadow, and held on firmly. Dominic shook his head as he tried to see clearer, but he could not hold on to the strings and the moment was gone.

"Are you okay, Mr. Gray?" Dominic raised his eyes and saw that both father and son were staring at him with a mixture of concern and curiosity.

Dominic forced a smile and nodded. "Of course I am, yes, yes."

"Okay, want to go through the Timeline together? We just got here and have not gotten around to seeing much. I just saw you the moment we stepped in," Eric offered.

"Sure, let's do that," Dominic smiled.

They moved into another section and Dominic's smile suddenly froze on his face when he saw the first display. It was a picture of a beautiful woman with brown hair, falling to her shoulders and brown eyes. He walked forward slowly and read the contents of the plaque, Mirabel Cooper, 1977 to 2000. Dominic shook his head and ran a hand through his hair crazily. What on earth was this madness? He backed away, unable to fathom what he was seeing. It was not possible.

I met her just last weekend! I exchanged messages with her two days ago! How on earth is this possible?! He screamed internally.

A squeak caused Dominic to turn to his side to find Eric's father's eyes frozen on the picture too. The man was sweating even though the library was very cold.

"Are you well, dad?" Eric asked his father, placing an arm around his shoulder.

The man shook his head and the dazed look was gone from his eyes.

"Of course.. why… won't I be?" He stammered.

Not paying them any attention, a heavy-hearted Dominic turned back to the picture. Surely, this had to be a mistake. His heart was pounding in his chest, and he could feel himself getting hot. Maybe it was her mother? Or her sister? Maybe it was someone she was named after and looked like so much. Maybe…?

No, no maybes. This was crazy! His eyes flitted over the plaque, and he picked up some words, 'Author', 'Chief Editor, Doverston paper'. Dominic shook his head. He could not read any more. It made absolutely no sense!

He turned around and hurried out of the library. Faintly, he heard Eric calling out to him but he ignored it. He could not think straight now, and he needed answers right away!

"Hey, Dominic, I did not know you were coming here, else I would have asked that we come together," Mrs. Potts bumped into Dominic at the door.

"I do not have the time to talk, Mrs. Potts. I will see you later."

Not waiting to listen to her, he dashed off. Dominic made it to his car and started the engine. Immediately, he pulled out of the parking lot and headed toward the back road. He did not have over thirty minutes to waste heading to her house. He needed answers right now.

The sun was still up when Dominic was making his way down the cracked road to Mira's home. The sight in front of him caused him to step on the brakes suddenly, and he jerked forward. Dominic's mouth fell open.

"How… how is this possible? I was here, I was here last, last weekend!"

Dominic alighted the car and moved closer to the building before him. Gone was the warm and inviting home he had seen and slept in! Now, he was staring at a house that was a shadow of its old self. It was clear to him that it used to be more beautiful. He had seen a glimpse off that the last time he was here. This was so crazy! Unbelievable! Now the yard was overgrown with tall grass, blocking a lot of the entrance. The paint was peeling, the building was cracking and the previous tended to vines had overgrown and twisted around the windows, most likely sealing them shut.

Gingerly, Dominic made his way to the building. His eyes widened when he saw some faint yellow strips stuck in the grass. He could barely make out the words 'cross'. Dominic turned to the door and he tried to open it but it was stuck. A few more attempts of kicking and pushing later, and he found himself standing in a dusty and musky place that had clearly not seen sunlight or air for years.

"Mira!" Dominic called out, alarm rising is his chest. Please let it not be you, he thought to himself.

While what his eyes were seeing should have been enough to convince him of what he had come here to find out, he blatantly refused to accept it. There was no way he could accept that Mirabel was dead, and had died a long time ago. Then, who did he see? Surely, he had to be dreaming.

Dominic headed to the kitchen and he froze at the sight of a faded white outline on the floor. It was shaped like a curled up human body, and had obviously been there for a long time. Dominic had watched enough movies and read enough books to know that the place had been a crime scene and the outline was that of a dead body. He shut his eyes and fought back the tears. Had she been killed here? In her own home? A place that was supposed to be her safe space? Maybe this was why she had never left. But how could all these crazy things happen? And where on earth was she now? Did she know he was coming? Had she left because of him.

Dominic ran a hand through his hair in frustration. He was totally drained. The more questions he asked, the more kept pouring out. He stood up and as determinedly as he could, Dominic made his way to the rest of the house. He searched every nook and cranny where a human could hide, or rather, a ghost but found nothing. As he moved through the house, he called her name and was greeted with an echo. Even the light bulbs no longer worked. He blinked and slapped his head with a palm. He had no idea what was going on. All he knew was that he was going crazy because of it.

Dominic stood up, and headed out of the house tiredly. He stood next to his car and looked back at the house. Twenty-three years, she had been dead for twenty-three years! Had she been roaming for that long? He held his chest as his heart broke for her. Some of the things she had said were beginning to make so much sense to him now.

Dominic had no idea how he made it to his home, but he did as thirty minutes later, he found himself sitting in his car in the driveway, crying as his heart ached. The more he thought about it, the more pain he felt, and he could not even explain why.

CHAPTER SIXTEEN

THE MAN'S EYES were frozen on the screen as he watched and waited. It had been hours since he sent the message and so far, he had received no response from her. He had not been holding his breath, but rather, he has been holding on to a sliver of hope, that maybe, just maybe she would reply. But who was he kidding? The man sighed and held his head in his hands. He was going crazy and he had no one he could tell all of these to. They were probably going to think she was crazy, maybe some after effect of the accident. He sighed and lifted his eyes up.

"Twenty-three years," he whispered. "She was 23 years old when she died. I wonder what happened that she died so young.:

Dominic's buzzing phone caused him to jerk in shock. He sighed and turned off the alarm. The man shut his laptop as he stood up. There was no point sitting and waiting. She was nor going to reach out to him. He had to accept the truth, a truth he could not tell others, that his ghost-writer was actually a ghost. Crazy things were happening indeed. Things that were absolutely inexplicable.

Dominic retired to bed that night, a very troubled man. His dreams were plagued with flashes of Mirabel Cooper and he found himself awake for a good part of the night till morning.

Once the day was bright, Dominic jumped out of bed, had a shower and headed out of his house. He had one destination in mind, Ian's.

Ian looked up from the customer he was attending to at the sound of the jingling bell that announced Dominic's arrival.

"I will be with you soon," he mouthed to Dominic.

Dominic nodded and settled at a table. He picked up the menu and stared at it, barely making out the words spread across it. Moments later, his friend approached him but he was oblivious to his presence, as he continued to stare at the menu blankly.

"The menu must look very delicious seeing how you cannot stop staring at it," an amused Ian said.

Dominic sighed and looked at his friend, "You are done."

"You know, I really should not be talking you right now, man, after what you did."

"What do you mean?" Dominic asked with a raise of his eyebrow.

"Don't tell me you have already forgotten WHT happened just last night. Not only did you leave me alone with the ladies, you also left the party early without even letting me know."

"Oh that," was all Dominic said with a slow nod.

"Wow, I see that is all you have to say." Ian frowned as he settled into the seat across Dominic's. Ian tilted his head as he studied his friend. "You look a mess. Didn't you get any sleep last night?"

"No, I didn't," Dominic answered honestly.

He smiled gratefully at the server who brought him his regular cup of iced tea just then.

"How come? You left pretty early. Or wait a minute, didn't you go home? I knew it! Who is the lucky woman?"

Dominic shook his head as he said, "I am not doing this with you."

Ian scoffed, "sometimes, you can be a killjoy, you know."

"I thought that was no longer news," a quiet Dominic replied just before he took a sip of his tea.

"Fine, keep it to tell yourself." Ian rolled his eyes, "But remember that nothing is hidden under the sun. Whatever you are hiding will come to light someday."

Ignoring his friend's words, Dominic said, changing the subject, "The timeline event yesterday, at the library, is it the first of its kind?"

Ian quirked a brow, "That is a swift change of topics. Are you trying to distract me from pulling the truth out of you?"

Dominic stared exasperatedly at him, causing Ian to roll his eyes, "Fine, fine, way to kill the vibe. No, okay? It is not the first. It's something of a once in four years thing. This should be the third of its kind. It started I think, 2015? I forget."

"I see..." Dominic said slowly. "And it is always the same thing? O mean, the same people."

"I don't know, I never really get involved that much. This is actually the first I am attending. I was not in town during the last two."

"I see..." Dominic nodded slowly. "So uh... who handled all the collections? You know, I mean, the pictures, and all the historical stuff? Do they belong to the library?"

"Oh not all, some come from the archives and others are loaned by people in possession of them, for instance, their family members. Why all these questions, Dominic? Are you suddenly interested in management of the local library?"

"No, no," Dominic shook his head. He was trying to think of a way to be honest and get the knowledge he sought, but at the same time not be considered a mad man. "One of the exhibits, or rather people in the timelines, she is an author too. I was just curious about her."

"She huh?" Ian tapped his chin. "Doverston has produced a food number of female authors. Who could you be referring to?"

"Uh..." Dominic acted as if he was trying to recall the name, to prevent showing how much he was bothered by it, and to also find out how much his friend knew, "Mirabel... something, I think it started with a 'K' or a 'C'. I cannot recall her last name."

Dominic watched his friend as the man's brow furrowed as he scanned his memory.

"Mirabel, Mirabel, wait a minute, you must be referring to Mirabel Cooper."

"Oh yes, that's it. Do you know her?" Dominic asked quietly, trying to hide how great his interest was.

"She is dead, man. Didn't you see it? She died in 2000 or something," Ian said with a deep frown.

"Oh yes I recall I did. She was quite young though, only Twenty-three," Dominic commented, trying to infuse nonchalance into his voice.

"Uh huh," Ian said quietly as he motioned to the menu in Dominic's hands, "Aren't you going to order?"

"Yeah, sure, sure. I'll have the garlic and chicken pasta. So… uh… how did she die? That was young. She have an accident?"

Ian sighed and stared pointedly at Dominic, "Look man, people do not like talking about what happened to Mirabel Cooper and for good reason. Her death was a blow to Doverston. I was just a kid then but I saw how devastated my parents were. The Coopers and Woods were kind to them and for Mirabel to die, it broke the hearts of many."

"You still haven't said how she died, man." Dominic pointed out quietly.

Ian shook his head, "She was murdered okay?"

"Whoa. That's… that is…" Dominic's eyes widened as he was genuinely shocked. He had suspected based on the signs he had seen at the house but to have it confirmed, it was heartbreaking. "Right here in Doverston?"

"Nope," Ian shook his head. "It happened at one of her family's properties a town over."

"So what happened to the rest of the family?"

Ian shrugged, "I don't really know. I don't think there are any more Coopers seeing how it was Amelia who was in charge of the Woods' and Cooper collection. I heard her discussing with the Librarian about when they will be returned."

"Amelia?" Dominic asked.

"Amelia Woods, man, old man Gerald Woods' first child. Come on man, do you really know nothing about anyone in this town?"

"I don't think I do…" Dominic said slowly.

"Anyway, I am not surprised that she is the one in charge of whatever is left of the two estates, Woods and Cooper, and trust me, there is not much left. Those two families were not treated well after the death of the patriarchs and…" Ian's mouth suddenly clamped shut. He was wearing a look that Dominic interpreted as one from someone who just realized he had said too much.

"What do you mean by they were not treated well?" Dominic pushed.

His friend threw him a cold look and said, "Drop it man. Drop it. I would really like us to stop talking about this now."

"Okay, man. I hear you. I was just curious, is all.. you don't have to get aggressive." Dominic made a point of rolling his eyes, then shook his head. "Can I have my food now?"

Ian threw him one last look before he stood up and headed out. Dominic watched him, a myriad of thoughts running through his head. He had no idea who Amelia Woods was but he knew very importantly, that he needed to find her. If she was the only connection to Mirabel that was left in the world, it was imperative he did. He could hope that she gave him audience though.

Whoever she was, she most likely resided in Doverston. Dominic knew he could not ask Ian for more information. He had oy managed to extricate the little he got and he could tell that his friend had become tight-lipped. He would have to think of another way, that was for sure.

His meal arrived a little while later and as he ate, Dominic kept running several scenarios through his head, trying to see if any of them would work. The man was exhausted but he had to keep going.

"Hey Dominic, my man. Why do you sound so exhausted? Aren't you supposed to be on some long indefinitely vacation?" That was Wesley's greeting when Dominic called him later that day.

"Sleep has been eluding me these past days, I cannot lie," Dominic admitted.

"That is too bad, man. I thought it was getting better. You still seeing that therapist?"

"I started seeing a new one out of town a month ago," Dominic told him.

"Time, man, that is what you need, I am sure with time."

"I can only hope, man, but I will be honest with you, I do not feel very positive."

"I understand, but give it time. You almost died, man. It's understandable that your mind is trying to process a lot of things."

"I'm not so sure what's going on anymore," Dominic said quietly.

"What was that? I didn't hear you," Wesley prodded.

"Uh, nothing important. Look, I need Alex's help."

"Oh? Give me a second." In the background, Dominic heard his friend calling out to his wife. In a moment, he could hear Wesley clearly again, "Hey, man. You are on loud speaker, Alex is here."

"Hey Dominic, you okay? Someone bothering you?"

Dominic heard his friend laugh, and say, "That your default?"

"Hey no one is allowed to bother our friends and family. You know that," Alex said, causing Dominic to smile and Wesley to chuckle.

"Thanks Alex, but this is actually not a call for that kind of help. I need to find about something that happened some years ago. I haven't had much luck retrieving anything online. Maybe it's because it's been so long, or who knows if everything about it was plugged."

"Oh really? Well, nothing is ever hidden completely? What are the details you have? Let me see what I can dig up."

"It's a murder case from 2000."

There was silence on the other end, and then, Wesley exclaimed. "Murder? What are you getting yourself involved in over there man?"

"Nothing crazy, okay? I just would like to know more about this. Look, it's a twenty-three-year-old woman, Mirabel Cooper. She is from Doverston but was killed on her family property in Ravetown. I know, I know you think…"

"Dominic…" this was Alex. "Are you sure everything is okay? Finding out about a murder from over two decades ago, this is not the kind of request that is spurred by nothing."

"I really just need the information, Alex. Can you help me?"

She sighed and said, "Sure, I will see what I can find in the next week."

"Thank you very much. I really do appreciate this."

"Please be careful, Dominic," that was the last thing from the couple before they hung up.

His phone hanging from his hand, Dominic headed to his room window that overlooked the street and looked out. From the corner of his eyes, he could see the shadow behind Mrs. Potts' Curtain. He shook his head slightly. He had not seen the woman since that night at the library, but he had noticed her peeping. If she had something to say, she was keeping it to herself and he was glad about it.

But she might know something, a voice said in his head, causing Dominic to groan inwardly due to its accuracy. Mrs. Potts had been around for a really long time and she was certainly a gossip. She could be someone who could shed some light on this mystery he had found himself embroiled in.

Why exactly am I worrying about this issue? He found himself thinking. Because it does not make any sense. I have been thrown headfirst into a situation I do not understand or have any control over. I have to grasp at the straws I can find, and dig as much as I can to find any answer that would lead me to a solution maybe the solution lies in what happened to Mirabel. whatever it is, i just cannot step back and pretend that the last months never happened. I have to find her, I have to get my answers, Dominic thought determinedly.

He turned away from the window and headed down the stairs and out his front door. Dominic sat in the front seat of his car for a while, contemplating what he had to do next. He needed to find Amelia Woods, but how he was going to do it was the question. It was not like he could just bluntly ask anyone who she was. Well, why not? It would be one of two things. It was either he got an answer or did not get an answer. But he was worried about raising alarm. That was another thing that bothered him indeed. Maybe he should have asked Alex to find her? Nah. He shook his head. That would only be drawing more questions. He had barely managed to convince her about digging into Mirabel's murder case. If they thought there was something more to it, things were bound to get very complicated.

Dominic pulled out of his driveway with one destination in mind. He would start from there and see what he could find.

The man headed into the library, looking around as he searched for the head Librarian. She had to be somewhere around.

"Hey Dominic, what brings you over here? Looking for some good books?"

Dominic turned around to see one of the deputy librarians. He smiled as he said,

"Hey, Cassie. Is Mrs. Burns around?"

"Oh no, sorry she's not. Her daughter has the flu so she had to go over there to take care of the kids. I don't think she will be back till the weekend. You need her assistance? Is it something I can help you with, per chance?"

"Uh… I don't know. I actually…" Dominic hesitated and looked around, to confirm that no one was within hearing distance. "I am actually looking for someone."

"Oh? And you came to the library. Hmm…. Is this person a patron?"

"I really gave no idea."

Cassie crossed her arms as she said, "You are going to have to give me more than that, Dominic. I cannot help you if you give no information."

"Well, you see, I am looking for Ms. Woods, Ms. Amelia Woods."

"Ms. Woods… Amelia Woods…" Cassie repeated. She started saying, "I don't think I…"

The woman suddenly burst into laughter, "Oh my goodness, wait, is it Amelia you are calling Ms. Woods? You are really super polite, Dominic. What they say are certainly not lies."

"I don't understand," a confused Dominic asked. The woman certainly looked very amused and he could not figure out why.

Still chuckling, the woman said, "You are looking for Ms. Amelia Woods, right? Go over to BookADrink."

"BookADrink? The café close by?" Dominic asked. He had not been there since the first day several months ago. "Does she usually hang our there or what? She's a patron?"

Cassie smiled and nodded. Her eyes twinkled as she said, "Yes, sure. That's it."

"Thank you, Cassie."

Dominic turned around and headed out of the library, in the direction of the café. He stepped in and was once again greeted by that ambiance that enveloped you in a warm hug. His eyes followed the Ferris wheel pattern, once again enthralled by it. He had no reason for not returning all this time even though it had always been at the back of his mind.

It was because of her, that was for sure. The thought ran through his head the moment he saw the beautiful woman. She always left him with his heart racing and that had made him quickly build a fence and dun as far as his legs could take him, not looking back. He had been hurt enough by loving Angelica. His subconscious had taken charge and he had put as much distance as he could between himself and this woman because he knew she completely captivated him. Twice they had met already and he always found himself entranced. He was not willing to take that chance and had backed away. Now here he was again, in her territory, trying to find someone very important.

He swallowed hard as she got closer to him. Her luscious locks were held up in a high ponytail. She stopped in front of him and said with a soft smile

"Welcome to BookADrink. What service would you like today?"

"Uh… I am actually looking for someone. I was told I will find her here," Dominic explained, his eyes looking everywhere but at her.

"Really? Who is this someone you seek?"

"Ms. Amelia Woods, do you know her?"

The woman's brow went up higher and she was visibly taken aback for a second. She quickly regained her composure but her reaction lasted long enough for Dominic to know that he was on the right path.

"Is she here?" He pushed forward.

"What do you want with her?" The woman asked, now eying him suspiciously.

"Well…" Dominic cleared his throat. "It is a little confidential."

"Then I cannot help you," She was about to turn around when Dominic called her,

"Wait." He sighed and looked around. His voice went down am octave as he said, "I want to talk to her about Mirabel Cooper."

The woman's eyes blazed with anger. "You are one of those slimy reporters after highlights and fame."

"No, no, of course not."

"Oh really?" She snapped. "You come in here looking all fancy asking to see someone you don't even know, about something that is none of your business and you expect me to be fooled? I am sorry to disappoint you, sir, but I am nor buying whatever you are selling. Leave now and don't return."

"Please, it's really urgent I see her," Dominic insisted.

"Well, it is a shame that I do not care." The woman was quick to reply.

"How about you ask her and see what she says? If she still does not want to see me, I'll take a bow."

Just then, a voice caller from near them.

"Hey Amelia, the new menu is to die for, absolutely delicious. You will make Mr start coming here every day."

The woman flashed him a smile and turned back to a stunned Dominic.

"You are Amelia Woods?" He managed to ask.

"Now that you know, do see your way out, all right?"

She turned and headed off, not sparing him another glance.

Sighing, Dominic left. He settled behind the wheel and tapped it with his finger as he waited. She has been in front of him all long. Wow! It was no wonder Cassie had been so amused when he asked about her. And she had not even bothered to correct him impression. The man shook his head. She probably was having lots of fun with him. Dominic looked at the door of the café and sighed. He had to do something. He had to convince her that he was up to no good, but what could he possibly do shy of telling her he had been in constant communication with her dead family friend? That was bound to make things worse and she would most likely kick him to the curb. He had to think of something else.

Dominic leaned backward and shut his eyes, hoping for some inspiration.

When he opened his eyes later, he almost jumped. He was surprised to find that it was already dark. Daytime was only a few hours ago. How…? He shook his head. He was absolutely exhausted and really could not think straight.

A tapping sound pulled Dominic's attention to his side. He swallowed hard when he saw Amelia on the other side. She motioned for him to come out, then, straightened. Gingerly, Dominic alighted the car, turned around and went to stand beside her.

"What are you still doing here?" She asked softly.

"I need to see you."

She rolled her eyes, "For someone who claims he is not a reporter, you sure do act like one. You are not helping your case in the least bit, with your lingering."

"I am very sorry you feel that way. It is just very urgent that I see you."

She sighed and it looked like she wanted to say something bit seemed to think better of it. She shook her and said, "Fine. Let's go have dinner and you can tell me what is so impotent that you had to sleep in front of my cafe."

"Are you serious?" An examined Dominic asked.

"I am beginning to regret my decision," She said rightly.

"I'm coming, sorry, sorry." Domonic opened the passenger side door for her. Rolling her, eyes, she slipped in.

With mode verve in his step, and energy running through his veins, Dominic started the car. He could finally feel it, he was making progress. He had no idea what exactly he could find out from her but he knew that he was finally making a huge step. He could only hope that it was a step in the right direction.

Dominic intentionally did not take her to Ian's restaurant to prevent questions. Opting for a restaurant he had never been to before, the pair found themselves seated at a noodle soup shop a little while later.

"This is quite a cozy place," Dominic looked around.

"Uh huh, a lot of Doverston is cozy." Amelia said with a nod.

While they awaited their food, Dominic took the chance to finally get a closet look at Amelia. Her hair was now held back by a call clip and some wisps framed her face. She looked more beautiful than she did earlier. He quickly averted his gaze. Who was he kidding? He always thought she looked more beautiful than the previous time, every time he saw her. Dominic hid his smile behind his glass of water.

"Thank you," they appreciated the servers in unison once there meals arrived.

For a while, the only sounds that could be heard at their table were the satisfied slurps of the pair. Amelia was the one who broke the silence.

"So, what do you want to know about Mirabel?"

"Were you close to her?" She looked at him questioningly and he explained, "Your eyes, they softened when you mentioned her."

Amelia nodded, "Yes, I did know her. She was a big sister to all of us. Like, the age difference was over ten years, but she never treated us differently. She was sweet with a beautiful heart."

"Your dad and hers were close."

"Close is an understatement. They were more of brothers, you know.. the only thing they didn't do was stay in the same house." She sighed deeply. "For us their children, we received love double-fold, from both ends."

"I am very sorry. I heard about what happened to them. They died a year apart from each other. That must have been very devastating."

"Do you want to talk about my father or Mirabel? Why did you even reach out to me?"

"I saw the display at the Timeline history, and found out you were the one who loaned the belongings of the Woods' and Cooper family for the exhibition. I figured you are the closest living family left.

"You have said a lot of things, but still have not said anything," she said haughtily.

"Who would want to kill Mirabel? She was just twenty-three and from what I have heard, everyone loved her father. Everyone loved both of your fathers. Was it related to the business? Was it a robbery gone wrong? What exactly happened? And what became of your fathers' businesses? I know for a fact that Doverston paper no longer belongs to your family. Is this the same for the rest? And what exactly happened?"

She narrowed her eyes at him, "You say you are not a reporter but…"

"I am really not a reporter. Trust me, Mirabel. I mean you no harm."

"That is very hard for me to do, seeing how I have been burnt several times in the past," She said through gritted teeth.

"I… I don't know what to say."

"There is nothing you can actually say," She replied quietly. "Anyway, there is nothing I can tell you about what happened to Mirabel."

Dominic eyes followed her every move and when she spoke, he saw a hint of something he could not explain in her eyes. Guilt? Fear? Worry? He could not interpret it.

She took a sip of her black tea and said, "The businesses, let's just say that those who have more power took most of it."

"Those who have more power? What does that…?"

The soft gaze in her eyes had been replaced by a hard look and Dominic followed her eyes to find what she was focused on. The news was reporting on a mayoral candidate for the city. Dominic had been seeing his posters around town since he arrived, and from whispers he had heard while out in the market, lots of people had positive things to say about him.

"He is definitely going to lead in the polls," someone at the table next to them said, and his friend concurred.

Dominic heard a sudden sound and turned to see a tense Amelia glaring at the television. She was oblivious to the fact that her chopsticks had clattered to the floor.

"Amelia, are you okay?" he reached out for her but she jerked out of his reach.

"I have to go now, I can't be here."

She rose and he stood up quickly, "Let me take your home, at least. I promise I won't ask anything else."

"Fine," she bounded out of the restaurant and he hurried to catch up with her.

As soon as he pulled up in front of the five-story townhouse, Amelia muttered a goodbye and bounded out of the car. Sighing at how things had turned out, Dominic pulled away. He found himself at a red light and leaned back in his seat. As he tapped on his steering wheel, he could not help wondering about what happened at the restaurant. What exactly transpired between Amelia and the man? She had held so much anger in her eyes.

Drawn to music blaring beside him, Dominic turned to the side and found himself staring at a car with two men in the front seats. The back of the one in the passenger seat was to him. Dominic narrowed his eyes at the streaks of golden yellow in the man's hair. Where had he seen it before? Was it now some popular style? He wondered.

The car with the man pulled forward first and went ahead of Dominic. Dominic followed slowly behind as they were headed in the same direction. He quirked a brow when the car pulled into the parking lot of Groenig, the beloved mayoral candidate. Dominic crawled past and watched the men step out of the car. They did not look like the kind of people that had any business with someone supposedly as clean as Groenig. They looked like they would fit better working as henchmen for some gang leader. Stop judging people by their looks, Dominic. He quickly chided himself. He picked up speed and headed on to his home, his thoughts returning to Amelia and her strange reaction earlier.

A warm shower later, Dominic settled into his bed, and pulled his laptop close to him. His fingers flew across the keyboard as he searched up 'Steve Groenig'. Hundreds of articles popped up and for the next hour, Dominic skimmed through them, searching for anything that could direct him to what could have created animosity between Groenig and Amelia.

Dominic sighed and pushed his laptop away. The man was clean, in fact, it seemed like he was too squeaky clean. For someone who had been in politics for over twenty years, it seemed too good to be true. it was not like it was impossible, but to have no issue whatsoever? Nah. It did not sit right with him. It was as if someone had gone to great odds to make him look spotless.

Dominic had been a writer long enough to know that all was not always as it seemed on the surface.

He sighed and swiped over to his messages. As he had expected, there was nothing from Mira. There had been no message since he found out the truth.

"Where are you, Mira?" he said softly. "Why did you reveal yourself to me? I really don't know what to do. Help me, will you? Tell me what you want."

With a heavy heart, Dominic turned off the night light and turned in for the night.

CHAPTER SEVENTEEN

THE BOY WAS running into the woods, tears rolling down his cheeks. The sight of her, bleeding from her belly on the floor broke his heart but he had to keep running. She kept flashing in his head, her bleeding body. That was what she had told him. She had told him to run. He had to run. The man… the man with hair like the sun and face as haggard as one who was beaten by the sun, he had stabbed her. 'Run! Run!' He heard her voice in his head. A hand suddenly grabbed his shoulder and he screamed.

Dominic bolted awake, screaming at the top of his lungs. He gasped as he reached for his dream journal. As he wrote out everything, his hands shook. Dominic grabbed his empty glass and staggered down the stairs to get water from the kitchen. The man settled at his kitchen counter, nursing the glass with one hand, his other hand messing up his hair. The moonlight bathed him where he sat. He shut his eyes as memories of his nightmare flooded him. Mirabel bleeding from a wound, a boy running to save his life, a man with golden hair. Dominic sighed and took a large gulp of water. this was the first time that his nightmare was clear to him, and it was strange. The only person he could recognize in it was Mirabel. He had never seen the boy and the man before. Had Mira done this to him somehow? It was clear that something strange was going on. She was a ghost, she had made him see her, she had turned a desolate house into a mansion, and she had fed him! Who was to say she was not capable of infiltrating his dreams. But then, what did she want from him? And secondly, was she simply showing him what happened to her? Or were they actually his memories?

"How am I connected to all of these?" Dominic wondered aloud.

He had to do something. He jumped up and ran to his room. For the rest of the night, Dominic sat in front of his computer using a computer software to generate sketches of the man with golden hair and the boy. It was already past six am when he found himself staring at the complete sketches. And he was satisfied by them. Now, he just needed to ask his friends to help him find them. If his nightmares were the truth, that meant, it was this man who killed Mirabel, and he had killed the boy too, whoever he was.

Dominic sighed and ran a hand over his face. He had a long day ahead of him. The first thing on his agenda was finding out who Steve Groenig really was.

"Why come in, Dominic. It is a pleasure to see you." Ms. Ellen ushered him in.

"Thank you very much for seeing me on such short notice, Ms. Ellen." He smiled in appreciation.

"Oh that's okay. I certainly appreciate the company. I have tea and I have cookies. Which would you like to have? Both good for you?"

Dominic chuckled and said, "Sure, that is fine by me."

When they had settled down, Ms. Ellen smiled at Dominic and said, "You said you wanted to discuss something with me and you sounded quite urgent on the phone."

"Yes, yes, I did. I really hope you can tell me the truth about what you know, Ms. Ellen," Dominic started.

"I do not know what you are talking about but I definitely try to avoid falsehood, as much as I can, though I admit that I am not perfect. What do you want to know about, Dominic?"

He swallowed hard and said, "What really happened to the Woods and Coopers? You worked for the paper for so many years, even after the original owners died, so surely you know how everything unfolded. Can you tell me everything that you know?"

The woman sighed and she crossed her arm, "Why are you asking these questions, Dominic? Are you writing a book?"

"No, no. this is just something that has caught my attention and I would like to get to the bottom of it."

"I see…" She nodded slowly. "As you already know, Gerald Woods and Leon Cooper were best of friends. There was no rivalry between them and they raised the company and their families with love. After Leon died, Gerald never abandoned his family. Just as they had planned before Leon's death, Gerald brought Mirabel into the paper company as a chief editor. You see, that beautiful child had been interning at Doverston paper since she was fourteen. She knew the ins and outs of the company and everyone knew she was the perfect person to run the company. There was also no doubt in the mind of anyone that little Amelia would take over the bakeries when she was older. She had a flair for the culinary art you know. And that poor kid was following in the path of Leon and Mirabel so…"

Ms. Ellen's voice broke and tears rolled down her cheeks. She shook her head and said, "I am sorry, Dominic but I do not want to talk about this anymore today. I just cannot."

"I am so sorry for making you relieve such painful memories, Ms. Ellen. You don't have to talk about them anymore since it pains you so much. But can I please ask one last question?"

She stared at him. "What connection does Steve Groenig have to all of these?"

Her eyes blazed with anger. "That slimy bastard took away everything those poor children had with the help of his dirty friends at city hall."

"All I have been able to find on him are good things. Everyone is praising him, and looking forward to his tenure as mayor."

Ms. Ellen laughed mirthlessly. "The bastard has succeeded in whitewashing himself. He is certainly an expert at it. He did not waste time in swooping in even before the body was cold!"

Dominic climbed off the last step in front of Ms. Ellen's car and walked to his car slowly. If indeed Groenig had taken everything away, it would explain Amelia's anger. So now he knew a little more about the dynamics, but he was still no closer to finding out what had happened to Mirabel. Ms. Ellen had talked about Groenig swooping in even before the body was cold. Which had she been referring to? Gerald's or Mirabel's? When exactly had Groenig struck? He looked back at her door and sighed. He certainly could not go back in there now.

Just as he was about to enter his car, Dominic felt that tingling feeling in the back of his neck. It was a long time he had felt it, like he was being watched. His eyes darted around but he could see no one. Still, he was in a populated area, anyone who was staring at him could be anywhere. Deep in thought, he entered his car and drove to his next destination, BookADrink.

Amelia raised her head the moment she walked in. It was already five pm so the early crowd had already thinned out, soon to be replaced by the evening crowd. She quirked a brow as he walked toward her.

"What are you here for? To eat? Read or bug me?"

"Can it be all of the above?"

She scoffed, but he could see the hint of a smile in her eyes. "You can take table 10 then."

"Yes, ma'am," he said with a salute. She rolled her eyes, causing him to chuckle.

Dominic settled into a booth and pulled his notebook out of his pocket. He had drawn a schematic, trying to piece together the connections between Groenig and the Coopers and Woods.

"What are you doing?" A voice asked from behind.

Dominic jerked and looked up to find himself staring deeply into Amelia's eyes. She had snuck up behind him and had been looking over his shoulders.

He cleared his throat and quickly shut his book. "It is nothing."

"That does not seem like nothing." She grabbed the book before he could stop her and flipped through it, "What is all of these?"

Her eyes widened and she gasped, "Are you trying to find out who killed Mirabel?"

"Keep it down," Dominic whispered. His eyes flitted around, as he hoped no one heard her. there were a few customers spread across the space.

"Sorry, sorry," she whispered and she slipped into the booth across from him. Her eyes turned back to the book and he could see her surprise growing, "How did you get so much information?"

Dominic kept shut and turned to the window, to watch the children skateboarding outside.

"But I don't understand," her words pulled his attention back to her. Her eyes softened as she said, "Why? Why are you doing this? You have no connection to Mira. You didn't even know her."

"It is a bit complicated, and no, I am not writing a book, or doing some report. This is just something personal which I cannot explain. I do hope you believe me."

"I do believe you," she nodded slowly. "I can see the sincerity in your eyes and your actions. I always could, but I guess I am just too stubborn and scared to let anyone else in."

"You have never tried to find out what happened to her?" he motioned toward the book.

She sighed and ran a hand through her hair, "I was nine when it happened you know. Still reeling from uncle Leon's loss, dad's followed. And…"

She blinked back tears. "Mira was our strength, you know. She was hurt, so bad with everything, but she was determined to keep us going. She was going to keep the business moving and keep us together and would not let anything happen. You know, a few months after dad passed, she started working hard on something. I don't know what it was but it was enough to have her spend late nights. I started hearing more about this Groenig guy. He had hovered after Uncle Leon's death, but dad had put him in his place. He became a bother again when it was just Mira, but she was so strong, you know, she succeeded in keeping him out."

Dominic covered her hand with his and squeezed her hand. She smiled gratefully at him and took a deep breath. "I have no idea what Mira was working on before she died but I know she became more agitated. Then, I fell sick and I had to leave the country with my mom's sister to get treatment. It broke their hearts that they could not go with me but they had stay back and hold the fort. I left them behind, my family. And when I returned, it was all gone, Dominic. The only family I had ever known was gone. And Groenig, he was suddenly in charge of everything that belonged to our families. Can you believe it?"

"Them, when you say them… who are you referring to?"

"Mackenzie of course."

"I don't understand. Who is Mackenzie, Amelia?"

"Don't you know? He is Mira's younger brother. Mira was ten years older than him. Uncle Leon and his wife had Mira when they were still really young, and just out of high school. They had Mack ten years later after they got married, and my parents had me about four years after Mack. I was the baby of the house."

Dominic sat back in shock. In all his research, there had been no mention of another Cooper child. He tilted his head as he remembered what Ms. Ellen had been saying before she broke down. Had she been trying to tell him about the child? He shut his eyes as he remembered the boy who was running. Had that been Mackenzie? But why on earth would he be having dreams about Mackenzie? This was just so crazy.

"Hey, where is your mind at?"

"Um… Mackenzie, right? What happened to him? You… uh… said your family was gone."

She took a sharp intake of breath and nodded slowly, "He fell down the ravine at the house where Mira was killed. The police were never able to determine if it was an accident or if he was pushed."

"That's… I am so sorry, Amelia."

She sighed, "You know, coming back to find that the people I loved the most in the world were gone was a terrible blow. And then, few days later, Groenig comes with his court order, claiming our family owed him. He took every single thing from us, the bastard."

"I do not blame you for hating him as much as you do."

She chuckled, "Thanks for saying that, Dominic. You are a very nice person."

Dominic chuckled, "Well, you are singing a new tune. I am pleased to hear that."

"Whatever," she chuckled.

"Do you want a ride home?" he smiled at her.

"Well, I would like to have dinner first, then a ride home."

Dominic grinned wider, "Okay. I would like that too."

She tapped on the book and said, "And I want to help you out with this too. Back then, I was too weak to do something. I am no longer that weak nine-year-old. You cannot stop me."

"We have to be very careful. There is something Ms. Ellen said," he whispered to her. At that moment, Dominic recalled Ms. Ellen's words when she followed him to the door to see him out, 'My honest advice, Dominic? Stop digging. These people are capable of a lot of things. They have killed many before and they will not hesitate to do it again. they will do anything to get what they want, and to keep their secrets hidden."

"Killed many? What does that even mean?" Amelia whispered.

"No idea, but you need to know that things can get pretty dangerous. You already have a good life, you don't need to complicate it. I will never forgive myself if anything happens to you," Dominic whispered.

She smiled and patted his hand. "I will be fine. I should be thanking you for giving me the chance to find the answers to the questions that have been at the back of my head for so long.

Dominic sighed, "I really don't feel good about this."

"It will be fine," she winked.

CHAPTER EIGHTEEN

THE SOUND OF his doorbell pulled Dominic's attention from the sauce he was stirring.

"should I get that?" Amelia asked.

"No, it's fine. I'll get it," he smiled at her and headed to the door. He opened the door and his eyes widened at the people on his front stoop.

"Alex, Wesley, I… didn't know you were coming. Is everything okay?"

Alex pulled a solemn looking Wesley into the house and they shut the door behind them. Alex turned to him, worry on her face as she said, "Why on earth are you digging into a twenty-three-year-old cold murder case, Dominic and what connection do you have with it?"

"I am just trying to get answers for the poor girl who was killed so brutally," Dominic replied quietly. "Why do you guys look so bothered? What exactly did you find?"

"Dominic, are you sure about this? Because if you aren't, this is the time to forget about all of this," Wesley said quietly.

"What did you find?" Dominic asked them as he led them in.

"Hey, Dom, who was at the…" Amelia trailed off when she saw Wesley and Alex, whose mouths fell open. Amelia smiled softly and said, "Hi, I'm Amelia."

"Hi Amelia," the couple said in unison. "Alex here and Wesley here."

"Nice to meet you."

"Likewise," They spoke again.

Amelia chuckled, "Do you both always sync your words?"

"Only when we are stunned, and believe me we are stunned to find a woman in Dominic's home," Alex grinned.

Dominic rolled his eyes but that did not stop Wesley, as rubbing his hands in glee, he said, "Are you both dating? Are you his girlfriend?"

"Not yet," Dominic and Amelia replied in unison, and they burst into laughter.

"Well, they are both on the same page. That is good to know," Alex nodded slowly.

She looked at Dominic and Wesley. Amelia nodded, understanding the unspoken message.

"I am going to take my leave now. I have a ton of stuff to do. It was really nice meeting you both."

"No, you should stay, this concerns you too, Amelia." Dominic took her hand and led her to the sofa.

"Uh.. are you sure, Dominic?" she asked.

"Of course.

His friends looked at him questioningly and he nodded. The couple exchanged looks, shrugged and settled into their seats.

With a sigh, Alex slid a file across the table to Dominic. "This is the file from the station in Ravetown. As you can see, there is not much going on there. The killer or killers were never found and the case was never closed. Whoever killed Mackenzie and Mirabel Cooper is still at large, something I am sure you already know."

"This is about Mirabel?" Amelia gasped. She tried to reach for the file but Dominic backed away. He had just come across the crime scene pictures and there was no way in the world he was going to let Amelia see them. He shook his head slightly and she sighed.

Dominic blinked back tears. He felt an uncontrollable urge to cry at the sight of Mirabel lying lifeless. She had looked so vibrant when they met. How was this… how was any of this possible? Why did it even happen?

"There really is no new information."

"Was Steve Groenig investigated?" Amelia asked softly.

"He had an alibi," Alex explained. "And yes, he could have hired someone but that angle was not investigated. We have to remember that he became a sudden bigshot and started his climb into politics at that time. No one dared touch him with how corrupt it all was back then. Nothing else stands out, Dominic."

"Yet, there is something you are not telling me, something that is not on the file," Dominic said quietly.

"It's just the testimony of the first officer on the scene, it just does not make any sense."

"What do you mean?" Dominic asked. "And wait a minute, how exactly were the police alerted to the scene."

"For some reason we don't know, the killer shot a gun. Someone heard it and called the cops/ The officer said after coming across the body, he went on the grounds and found the body of the little boy had rolled down the ravine. He had been shot and it was already too late for him."

"O…kay, that seems plausible."

"Get this, it was a dark night all right? The property was not lit and even the other officers had an issue finding the house despite their front lights, and here is an officer who found a body at the bottom of a ravine with a small flashlight."

"You think he might have been a part of it?"

"I don't know what to think, but something is definitely fishy about his testimony."

"What is his name?" Amelia asked as she reached for the file.

"Pierce Gray," Alex informed them.

"What?" Dominic froze, "Did you just say Pierce Gray?"

All eyes turned to him. "Yes, he Is the first responder."

"What on earth is going on?" Dominic asked more to himself than to anyone else.

"What is wrong, Dominic?" Amelia placed a hand on his shoulder.

"Pierce Gray is my father," he said quietly.

"What?" the other three gasped.

"Wait a minute, Wesley said your father was a detective, but in New York."

"Exactly! In New York!" Dominic jumped to his feet and ran a hand over his face. He placed an arm on his hip as he paced, "I grew up in New York, and all my life that was where I have been. We never moved. And my mother, I asked her if she had ever been over here and she told me never! How is it possible that she lied to me and why did she even lie to me?"

"Well, maybe it was not a lie," Amelia started, "Maybe they had a long-distance relationship?"

"Yes, that could be it," Alex added.

Dominic scoffed, "My immediate younger sister was considering a long-distance relationship with an ex and you know what my mother said? she said she could not advise her from her experience because she never had to be away from my father."

"So she was with him wherever he went," Amelia finished his thought.

"She tried so hard to keep me away from here, and she is still trying. And I do not know why! What exactly is she hiding? How on earth am I entwined in all of these?"

"I am sorry I cannot answer your question, man. I think that…" Wesley's words were interrupted by a crash as a paper wrapped rock was thrown in through the front window. The three of them ducked while Alex was on her feet immediately and making her way to the door, staying in the shadows. She ran out just in time to take a picture of the license plate. She sighed and went back inside.

"Is everyone okay?"

"Uh huh. What was that?" Dominic stood up and dusted Amelia's hair, "Are you okay?"

She nodded and he kissed her cheek. They headed to where Alex and Wesley were standing, staring at the rock which was lying in the midst of glass. Alex slipped on a pair of gloves and picked up the paper.

She read out, "The next time, it will be a real bullet. If you do not want to be pushing daisies, stop asking questions and digging into what you have no business with."

"You have stepped on the toes of some people with your investigation," Alex said quietly.

"This only motivates you more, right?"

"You got that right," Dominic frowned, his eyes blazing with anger. "If they are sending me threats, it means I am getting close and I will not let them scare me off. I will fight them with everything I have."

"You have a family who will go crazy if anything happens to you, Dominic, so remember that before you decide to do anything stupid."

"I think I know who killed Mirabel, guys, I mean, I think so. I just need to find out if he is actually a real person."

"What on earth do you mean?" Wesley asked.

"I will be back," Dominic said quietly and hurried out. He was back in seconds with his open laptop. First, he scrolled over to the computer-generated sketch of the boy from his dreams.

"Mackenzie…" Amelia whispered and her eyes clouded with unshed tears. "Why is his photo here?"

"I was right then. I think he is the one," Dominic said as he scrolled over to the next picture of the golden-haired man.

Alex's eyes widened and she pulled the laptop closer to her, "How do you know this, Dominic? How can you be so sure?"

"Would you believe me if I tell you I dreamed about it?" Dominic asked quietly.

"Dom…"

"I am very serious. My dreams recently, they have been an absolute mess of things I do not understand. I see a boy running, I saw Mirabel being killed and this man was the one who did it."

"Surely he cannot just be taken in based on your words that you saw him in a dream, Dominic."

"That is true but I cannot shake off this bad feeling. I am sure he is the one," Dominic said quietly.

"It is highly possible." Alex said quietly and all eyes turned to her.

"What do you mean?" Wesley asked as he settled down next to his wife.

"This guy, I have crossed paths with him a few times. They call him Eel because he is as slippery as one. He has been arrested for multiple charges but he keeps finding ways to get out of it. It is clear that he has connections to higherups."

"So no charge has ever stuck?" Amelia asked softly.

"None whatsoever. He is originally from Doverston, if memory serves me right."

Dominic pulled the laptop toward him and gasped, "I cannot believe I did not figure it out all this time. Damn!"

"What is it, Dominic?"

"This man, I saw him going into Steve Groenig's office a few days ago," he said as he remembered the night when he had found himself wondering why someone who looked so haggard would be going into the office of a public servant.

"Are you serious, Dominic?"

"Yes, I remember thinking that he looked completely out of place there. I cannot believe that I did not place the faces all this time. I guess I got caught up on so much and forgot some very important things."

"We have to tread very carefully. The fact that he was there could mean a variety of things.

"It certainly means that there is a connection between the two men," Wesley stated.

"That is very true," Alex said with a nod. Her eyes looked over the mess on the floor and she said, "We need to clean this up."

"Tell me about it," Dominic sighed and he got up. He moved closer to the gaping hole in the window and sighed. "They sure are creative."

"How can you be joking about this, Dominic?" Amelia frowned.

"I am not, all right? I just think we need to think of a way to tackle the problems that come our way. There is really no use dwelling on them, right? We just need to think of a solution and move on."

"They are going to hurt you, Dominic. You have become important to me too, and I don't want to lose you too."

Dominic smiled softly and pulled Amelia into a hug, "I am so glad to hear that. You are very important to me too. I will be fine, it will be fine, all right? Please do not worry about this."

When they finally pulled apart, Dominic turned to Alex and nodded, 'I think we know what we need to do. We have to find out everything we can possibly find out about this Eel guy. He holds the key to all of this. He is clearly hiding something. We just need to dig it up."

"Leave it to me. I will get all I can about him. And you, stay safe out here, all right? Do not do anything risky or go to any places you would not normally go to. It is now clear that you are being watched. We need to do a bug sweep of your house to confirm that they are not listening in on your conversations."

"They are that connected, huh?' Dominic sighed. The next few weeks were going to be tough. He knew that for sure.

"There is something we are forgetting," Wesley said quietly, and everyone looked at him, "From all you have said, babe, this Eel guy used to be something of a gun for hire. Even if he has his loyalties now, back then, he might not have been attached to anyone."

"In other words, we cannot just conclude that it was Groenig that had him do the work. It could have been one of his numerous employers," Amelia added, nodding slowly.

"Exactly. Back then he was an independent contractor, and whatever he is doing right now, he seems like he is some sort of boss."

"So it is important that we find out exactly what Mirabel was up to at the time. Finding out what she was working on, might lead us to what she found."

"So, we are working on the assumption that she was killed based on what she was working on. What if it was because of the inheritance?" Amelia asked, clearly bothered.

"I kind of having the feeling that there is more to this than the estates of Woods and Cooper. It goes beyond that. What happened to Mirabel was deeper." Dominic sighed and ran a hand through his hair. "I have several people I need to talk to if I am going to make sense of all of this. And one of those people is my mother. I need to find out how we are connected to all of this. It is just so strange that she never talked about this town and was so adamantly against it."

"Maybe she did not have good memories here," Amelia tried to excuse her. Dominic shrugged,

"Who knows? Anyway, first things first, I need to get this window changed. This is just so annoying," Dominic groaned.

"You both can follow up the clues around town, carefully please and we will follow Eel and see where he leads us. We can only hope that he leads us to something very productive, else it will be a clear waste of our time."

"That is for sure," Dominic said with a s low nod.

CHAPTER NINETEEN

"YOU ARE BACK," Ms. Ellen said when she saw Dominic at the door. she smiled brightly when she saw Amelia, "And you brought the young miss."

"Hello, Ms. Ellen. It has been a while."

Ms. Ellen patted Amelia's cheek lightly and led them into her house.

"It has been a while indeed. And the two of you, what are you up to? Don't tell me you are still running after this issue. I heard what happened at your place, Dominic."

Dominic nodded his head, "News does travel fast in this town. I do not know how I feel about it though."

The woman sighed and led them in. She turned to Amelia and smiled, "I am guessing he brought you as moral support and in the hopes that you will convince me to say what I nod."

Amelia nodded, "I believe that was his plan indeed." Amelia leaned forward as she asked, "Do you think it is going to work, Ms. Ellen?"

"We will just have to see then, won't we?" Ms. Ellen winked.

"Sure, sure, let's say if my charms work on you."

Ms. Ellen chuckled as she sat back in her seat, "Well they certainly worked on the young man seeing how he is completely smitten by you."

Dominic chuckled while Amelia exclaimed, "Ms. Ellen!"

"What lie have I said?" the woman chuckled. Her smile slipped and she suddenly said, "I do not have much more to tell you."

"I think you do, Ms. Ellen. I cannot shake off the feeling that you know more than you are letting on. You are clearly holding a lot of cards to your chest. Why don't you let some of it down? You might find that it might be relieving."

The woman sighed and clasped her hands together as she said, "What do you want to know?"

"What exactly was Mira working on before she was killed?"

Miss Ellen frowned as she crossed her arms. She swallowed hard as she said, "Why does that bother you? What business does it have with what happens to her?"

"I think you can answer that question yourself, miss Ellen. I think you've always known deep down that's what happened to Mira or related to her work. And we already know a lot about Mira. We know that even when her father and Mr. Gerald were still alive, she was already stepping on the toes of criminals in the government. Their deaths did not deter her. Some people may say it was because of the inheritance that she was killed, but I am not inclined to believe that it was more related to the work she was doing."

Miss Ellen looked from one to another and she said, "Are you both have certainly thought about this a lot. Fine, you are right that Mira was working on some high-profile cases before she passed. And, it is also possible that one of these cases led to her death."

"Is there a particular one that comes to mind right now, that you would like to mention?" it was Amelia who asked this time.

Miss Ellen looked hesitant, and they would only hope that she did not keep any more things to herself. "The cases that Mira was working on were cases that she devoted all her time and energy to. Mira was so smart, had a lot of integrity just like her father and was determined to help everyone who crossed her path that needed help."

"So what happened? There is a particular case in your mind that you want to tell us about. Please trust us."

The woman sighed and said, "Shortly before Mr. Gerald's died, the paper started receiving lots of complaints about a corporation that was taking over the homes of people and building substandard Homes as well. Several people had lost their families in loved ones in building collapses across Ravetown and Doverston. It was a very grand scheme, that would bring a lot of people down when exposed, from the contractors to the government officials who gave approval for the licenses, to the building inspectors, and so many more people. But most importantly, the owners of the company."

"That is crazy!" the pair exclaimed.

"Indeed it was! To make more money, they sacrificed quality and purchased substandard materials. The death toll was rising and Mr. Gerald knew he had to do something. He and Mira decided to produce an eight-part series revealing the crimes, the corruption and the deaths that the company and stakeholders were hiding."

"Such a series would have been a blockbuster. I presume you never got a chance to make it, right?"

"Right," Ms. Ellen said with a nod. "Mr. Gerald died and for a couple of months the series was shelved as Mira tried to navigate the new role she had found herself."

"She resumed after some time?" Dominic asked, to which Mira nodded in agreement with the question.

"Yes, she did. And in the course of her research, Mira discovered something even more sinister, a possible connection between your father's death and these people, Amelia."

Amelia shook her head in denial, "But it does not make sense. Dad died of a heart attack which occurred during a car accident where his brakes fell."

Dominic's ears suddenly twitched upon hearing Amelia's words. That sounded like exactly what happened to him.

"All is not always as it seemed, my girl. Mira was investigating all of these before her death. I am convinced that it was what caused her death."

"So you do not actually think it is Groenig."

"Oh, I hate Groenig, and he is a sorry excuse for a man. But I do think that he was not involved in Mira's death. He was always a coward, and all he could ever do was shout and climb up the backs of those in power."

"This company, can we get the name?" Dominic asked.

She looked reluctant for a moment, then she nodded and said, "Fine'. Ms. Ellen provided her with the name and they thanked her profusely.

""There is also something very important that you need to consider, and I ask that you ponder over it."

"What is that?" Amelia asked.

"Due to the hecticness and tension flying around, Mira decided to head to the house close to Ravetown. Only a few people knew about the house, and even less knew that she was headed there."

"Someone sold her out?" Amelia gasped.

"It is just a theory I have always nursed," Ms. Ellen said with a shrug.

"Who are the people who knew that Mira was heading to the house?" Dominic asked calmly.

"Myself, and the housekeeper Susan, as she had to clean the house since it had not been used in a really long time."

"It is a small list, that is good. So where is this housekeeper?"

Amelia frowned, "I just remembered that woman. She literally disappeared after Mira's death, with no trace."

"So she's missing?"

Amelia scoffed, "Far from it. I think she got out of town for some time after the incident but she must have returned several years ago because when I returned after my graduate program, that was the first time I ran into her in all those years. The moment she saw me, she fled in the other direction."

"Exactly, that is her forte. She tries to avoid everyone connected to her past," said Miss Ellen.

"That actually makes her more suspicious," Dominic observed, more to himself than to anyone else.

"Uh huh. We definitely need to find her and see what she knows," Amelia fumed.

"She is not going to listen to just anyone," Dominic rationalized, "We need to get backup."

"Back… oh…" Amelia nodded as she understood.

They thanked Ms. Ellen again and headed out. As soon as they were outside, Dominic placed a call to Alex.

"We need your help, Alex. I think we have stumbled on something big, but first, we need to find someone."

Dominic and Amelia settled down at a café to wait for the information from Alex. As they waited, they talked about everything but the current situation at hand. With the recent happening, they knew they could never be too sure who was listening to them.

Dominic's phone buzzed and he looked down to see an address. Moving as unbothered as they could, they headed out and straight to the car. By the time they were arriving at the address Alex had sent to them, they met Alex at the gate.

"Right on time," Alex said with a nod. "Let me lead the conversation, all right? You got that?"

"Yes, yes, we hear you," Dominic nodded, as did Amelia.

"Perfect."

The moment the door pulled open, Dominic gasped at the sight of the woman. It was the woman that had run off that day at the farmers market. Who would have thought? What a small world. He leaned forward and whispered it to Alex, who nodded and turned to the woman. She flashed her badge as she said,

"May I come in? I have a few questions to ask you."

The woman swallowed hard and motioned to Dominic and Amelia, "What about them?"

Amelia rolled her eyes and opened her mouth to speak when Dominic placed a hand on her shoulder and shook his head slightly, stopping her from going any further.

Alex nodded at them and headed into the apartment. The pair of them leaned against the wall, exchanging looks.

"I do not feel comfortable about this. If she has anything to do with this, the chances are higher that she will try to harm Alex."

"Relax, Amelia. Alex is a decorated officer with extensive experience. There is no way she can win over her, well, except she was bitten by a radioactive spider."

Amelia chuckled and nodded, "Fine, I will not worry about it."

"Perfect," he winked at her.

They had already started to lose track of the time when Alex emerged from the apartment. Behind her was a red-eyed and still sobbing Susan. She lowered her head and before they could say anything, she said, "I am sorry, so very sorry. It was never my intention to see Miss Mira get hurt. She was always so good to me."

"What do you mean by that apology? What did you do?" Anger flared in Amelia's eyes and Dominic pulled her back. He led the still fuming woman to his car and tucked her into the seatbelt.

"I understand how you feel, Amelia, but you have to take it easy, all right?"

"Fine," she said curtly but she looked anything but fine. Someone rapped on their window, and Dominic opened the door for Alex who slipped in. there was silence for a moment, then, Amelia apologized for her impulsiveness.

"It's okay, Amelia. I know this is very hard on you. You are already doing such a good job, all right?" she smiled reassuringly at her.

"What did she say?" Dominic asked quietly.

"She only told her brother about it. She never knew that he would go on to tell someone else, and all of that sort. She was very sad and she has been living quite a depressing life. I have no doubt that all this time she has been plagued with the guilt."

"Who is her brother?" Dominic asked quietly.

"Sam Dale."

Dominic shut his eyes tight and sighed. Why did it feel like he was running in circles? It felt like everyone he had met since he arrived in Doverston were finding their way back into his life, and not in a good way.

"Do you know the man?" they asked him.

He sighed and explained his connection to Sam Dale as they headed toward the man's house.

The smile on Sam's face slipped the moment Alex flashed her badge. He swallowed hard as he ushered her in.

"My son is away, we can talk for a while."

"Were you present when Mirabel Cooper was murdered?" Alex asked firmly.

The man's mouth gaped. He swallowed hard as tears clouded his eyes. "I have never been asked that question."

"There is a first time for everything, Mr. Dale. If you don't want to talk today, that is fine. We will still find out what really happened that night. The truth has been hidden for so long. You can help us unearth it, or not, but I must promise you that it is a secret you will not be carrying it to your grave."

The man ran a hand over his face as he said, "I am sorry, deeply sorry. Indeed I was present when Eel stabbed her. it was the three of us. After he killed her, we went after the boy."

"And you killed him," Alex completed.

"No, of course no. I could never kill a child. I led him to a foliage and begged that he stay there till we were gone. I was indeed very surprised to find out that he died. The poor kid."

"You realize that you are one of the people who killed Mirabel Cooper right? You might not have poked her with the knife but you stood idly by and watched it happen.

"We were only supposed to scare her, that's all," the man whispered.

"Will you be willing to testify against Eel and your other partners? It was twenty-three years ago but I believe you certainly have more information to give me. Let's begin."

While she was there, Alex made a few calls. By the time she was done, an unlabeled vehicle had come to pick Sam Dale up. One of such had already been dispatched to pick up his son.

At the back of the car, Dominic was holding on to the sobbing Amelia who kept repeating the word, 'Thank you'.

Alex turned to them and said, "I just got off the call with my friends over in New York. There are a few things that you would want to know. First, Eel has just been arrested."

Dominic sighed, "You said he gets arrested multiple times in a month and gets away with it. What is the difference this time around?"

"He has been arrested for murder. He was caught red-handed," Alex explained. "That with Mirabel's murder, he will be going away for a long time."

"Wow…" was all Dominic could say.

"There is more," Alex added quietly. Dominic quirked a brow.

"The person he killed… It is the wife of Charles…"

"Charles…. No… that's…" A memory suddenly flashed in Dominic's head, bumping into someone with golden hair at the Korean restaurant all those months ago. It had been Eel? Damn!

"Please don't tell me he had a hand in my accident…"

"Investigations are still ongoing but it is looking that way. It turns out that Eel has decades worth of evidence, recordings and tapings which he kept as his insurance. She smiled softly and patted Amelia's hand. "We will find the person responsible for your sister's death. If it is those people, they will have to pay for it without a doubt. You have my word."

"Thank you so much," Amelia sobbed and Dominic hugged her tighter.

A few hours later, with Amelia tucked away up in his bed, Dominic was seated in front of the fire in his living room, staring into space. He was oblivious to the fact that his friends had crowded around him.

"Hey, Dominic," they said softly. He looked up and smiled at them.

"Thanks for coming over you guys, when I need you the most."

"Dominic…" Wesley cleared his throat. "There is something you need to know, We really have no idea what to make of it but… we feel you should."

"What do you mean?" He looked from one to the other.

"So, Sam Dale swore that he never hurt the kid, Mackenzie. Rather, he hid him away from the others," Alex started.

"That does not make any sense. He was reported dead and…."

"No one else saw the body, Dominic," Alex said quietly.

"I don't understand. What does that even mean?"

"I was able to trace a few of your father's colleagues who arrived at the scene after he did. Your father was the only one who saw the body. He apparently retrieved it from the ravine by himself, wrapped it up and took it to the morgue. There is no record of an autopsy, unlike the case of Mirabel. All that is there is a death certificate.

Dominic stood up and started to pace, "What are you trying to tell me?"

"Your dreams, Dominic," Wesley started quietly, "Seeing that man, seeing the murder, running, and everything else you have told me. even the connection you feel to this city, what if? What if…?"

"I know what you are thinking but it does not make sense."

"Dominic, I think it is actually the only thing that makes sense in all of this. You need to find out the truth from your mother. Think about it, why is there so much secrecy surrounding their stay here in Doverston? It does not feel right. I know you don't want to accept it because it's way too much but maybe you should try keeping an open mind."

Dominic shook his head as he said, "I am going to bed. I am done with this conversation."

Not waiting for anything they had to say, he headed to his room refusing to think about any of it. Was she his sister? Was that why she had reached out to him? None of it made sense, it could not be.

CHAPTER TWENTY

IT WAS THE ringing doorbell the next morning that woke Dominic up. He sighed and pulled himself out of bed. He was in one of the guest rooms as Amelia had fallen asleep in his room, and Wesley and Alex in the other guest room. The doorbell continued ringing incessantly. Grudgingly, Dominic made his way down the hallway to the door. he gasped at the sight of his mother and sisters there.

The girls threw their arms around him while his mother watched from the corner.

"No one said you were coming," he managed to say, his eyes on his mother. What was the woman hiding from him? Why had she lied to him all his life? Had she lied to him? What could he really trust?

Dominic sighed and let his sisters lead him into his home.

"Well, you have a nice place here," Eva grinned.

"Wait, is someone in the kitchen?" Ana asked. Dominic's eyes darted toward the kitchen. He had not heard it at first. He hurried to the door but he was not fast enough because his sister jumped in. She winked at him as she said,

"Who is the beautiful lady, big brother? Are you not going to introduce your family to her?"

"Right…" Dominic said slowly, "Amelia, meet my sister.. outside there you will see my mother and immediate younger sister."

"I should say hi," Amelia said as she quickly pulled off her apron and let Ana lead her out to meet the others.

Dominic sighed and looked over the pancakes Amelia was making. He shut his eyes tight and sighed as he remembered the pancakes that Mirabel had prepared for him. Were they truly related? He sighed and ran a hand though his hair.

"Hey, Dominic, what are you still doing in there? Come join us!" Dominic's sisters called to him. Sighing he headed out, still very much deep in thought.

"It seems like you have a full house," his mother was saying, "Amelia here was just telling us that Wesley and Alex are here. It has been so long we got the chance to see them."

"You don't say," Dominic said quietly.

"Dominic are you okay?" his sister asked quietly.

"Uh huh. You do not look like your usual cheerful and bubbly self," Eva added.

Dominic kept quiet, refusing to say anymore. Before his mother could go on too, Wesley and Alex emerged at the top of the stairs.

"Wesley! Alex! My darlings!" his mother waved at them and they excitedly joined them in the living room."

"Mom, can I talk to you?" Dominic asked quietly. He needed to find out the truth now. There was no time to waste any further.

Everyone exchanged looks due to the sudden response. Only Wesley and Alex were in the know of what was happening.

Once the door closed behind them, mother and son turned to face each other. His mother smiled at him and Patted his cheeks.

"Oh my child, you are so lean now. Are you even eating at all?"

"I am eating fine, mom. Can I ask you a question? I will truly appreciate your honestly."

"Sure son, you do not need to ask so formally. Is something wrong?"

"Is this your first time in Doverstone?"

Dominic could see the cogs literally running in her head as she thought of the best way to answer the question.

Finally, his mother nodded and said, "No. Your father was stationed here some time ago."

"I see..." Dominic nodded slowly, "Is there anything you would like to tell me, mom? Anything that you think I should be aware of? Think carefully."

"I don't think there is any…" she drifted off as she saw the pain in his eyes, "You know already, don't you?"

"I need you to tell me what I need to know, mom. The truth please."

She sighed and said, "I am sorry, son. It just was not the kind of thing we could tell you especially given the situation. Your father found you roaming the woods and dazed the night your sister was killed. Who doesn't know the Coopers in these parts? Your father knew enough to know that you returning to your life would be your end."

"So…" Dominic fell heavily into a patio seat, his head in his hands. He was oblivious to the fact that the others were staring at all of them from the other side of the house.

"I am sorry, son. I am so sorry. We had to sneak you out of Doverstone the next day and we decided that we would never return. It was the only way we could think about to protect you."

"Mackenzie?" Dominic raised his head to see a tearful Amelia. She pulled him into a tight hug. He looked back to find his sisters also teary eyed. Alex and Wesley must have figured out from his reaction that their suspicions were correct and had broken the truth to them. He was glad. He did not possess the strength to break the news to them.

"You will always be our big brother and nothing is ever going to change that," the girls said when they finally got their chance to hug him. Dominic finally pulled his mother into another hug. "Thank you for saving me instead of leaving me to freeze to death in the cold. Thank you for taking me like one of yours."

"I love you, son."

"I love you, mom. I love all of you."

A scream drew their attention back to the house and caused them to run to it.

"What's wrong Alex? Everything okay?"

Alex was pointing at the television where the news was displayed. Amelia gasped as she saw Eleanor in handcuffs.

"Isn't that that bigshot philanthropist?"

"Apparently, she is the mastermind behind Maribel's murder and the owner of the company Ms. Ellen told you about," Alex exclaimed.

Dominic shook his head, "Indeed all is not always as it seems."

That night as he slept, the blurry amusement park dream finally became clear to Dominic. It was as if the scales had suddenly fallen off. He saw him and his sister running around the park, their laughter as loud as their shrieks. The young boy found a seat next to a carousel and he settled in while his sister sat next to him.

"Did you know from the beginning?" Dominic asked his sister in his dream.

"I suspected as you look a lot like our father, but not till you said the ear cake, did I know for sure that you are my Mackenzie."

"I am sorry I could not be there with you during your last seconds."

"No, thank you my little brother, thank you for surviving. I can go in peace now that I know you are safe, truly safe. I love you, brother. Goodbye."

"I love you, sister, goodbye" he whispered.

A tear rolled down his cheek as Dominic finally slept peacefully for the first time in a long time.

A few monds later Dominic was doing a speech and book signing in a church he told the crowd how blessed he was to be an author and what it means to have a loving family, after all the usual talks and meet and greets he was drawn back into the empty church by this peaceful feeling.

She was there waiting for a last hug and goodbye
blow kisses as she faded into the mist............

MORE AMAZING BOOKS FROM THIS AUTHOR

COMING SOON!!

AMAZING PAGE-TURNING (ROMANTIC) THRILLERS

The Murder Academy (*Thriller Series*)

The Deadly Admirer

Author Website:
www.authormartin.com

AND BUSINESS BOOKS

Turning daily struggle into opportunities

How Passion can make a Business

AND ALSO, COMING SOON:

Define capital within your business.
(Online) Courses of these books will also become available.

ABOUT THE AUTHOR

My name is Martin van Helden (post grad MBA) Author
of amazing (Romantic) Thrillers and business books.
My long history of owning several businesses and
Doing a lot of research has given me the unique
Opportunity to write these amazing and entertaining books.
Martin has a passion for (thriller) mysteries with a certain
Depth in the storyline, and he has written
other compelling books.
He likes these books to be a source of entertainment and
encouragement for people to get the best out of your life.